THE RING

THE RING

SARAH ANNE CARTER

This book is dedicated to all the children who grew up missing a parent, to all the parents and siblings who grieve for their family members, and especially to the military spouses who chose to love someone who paid the ultimate sacrifice for his or her country. They and you will never be forgotten.

To help support Gold Star Families, visit
www.americasgoldstarfamilies.org.

To help support a Fisher House, visit
www.fisherhouse.org.

CHAPTER ONE

Amanda woke up and instinctively rolled over to Lucas' side of the bed. He wasn't there, and loneliness washed over her once again. Her eyes teared up a little, as they seemed to easily do when he was gone. It had been almost three months now. She heard her alarm go off and rolled back to her side of the bed to turn it off. Her thumb brushed against her ring finger as she touched the alarm button and realized her wedding ring wasn't there.

"No!" she yelled as she sat up, remembering, and let the tears flow freely.

Her wedding ring wasn't just a piece of jewelry bought from a store. It was a unique band created by her husband that blended all aspects of their lives. Three rings were twisted together to make one: There was a gold band from Washington State where she was born, a silver band from Charleston where Lucas grew up, a white gold band from Turkey where he said he was when he realized he was absolutely in love with her. A few months after the wedding, they got the engagement ring soldered

1

to her wedding ring so that it was one ring. She wanted to make sure she didn't lose either one.

But, last night, she was so mad he wasn't there to help her with the move that she had taken her ring off and flung it into their closet, which was full of boxes stuffed with his things. She would have to find it today. Yet, today was the last day she had to sort through the house before the packers came tomorrow. She still had the kitchen and office to sort through. She pulled herself together by taking some deep breaths. This time next week, she'd be back in Washington State where she knew the people, places, and streets – the place that felt like home. She just had to get through this move. She had done it once before when the military had sent them from Tacoma to Charleston and thought she knew what to expect.

"Okay, Amanda, you can do this without asking for help. Two more days and you can leave this state. Make coffee, do the kitchen, do the office, and then find the ring tonight," she said out loud to herself and got out of bed. A few last tears escaped and then she shook her head. The rest of her tears would have to wait.

CHAPTER TWO

A few years earlier ...

The morning rush was over, and Amanda was cleaning her glasses off on her maroon smock when the bell above the door chimed the arrival of another customer. Her co-barista, Jodie, had just gone to the back for her break. They took turns, and today was Jodie's turn to go first. Amanda put her glasses back on and looked up, ready to smile and greet the customer with the usual "Good morning! Welcome to Coffee First," but paused for a moment when she saw a man her age. She normally saw older men in their suits, khakis and polos, or military uniforms stop by the shop and a lot of women, but not young men. He looked like a college student, but he was wearing a military flight suit.

Coffee First was located just a few hundred yards from an entrance to Joint Base Lewis-McChord in Tacoma. The greater Seattle area was the land of coffee shops, and there was a drive-thru one right across the street and another one even closer to the gate. However, both of those were known to have baristas who wore revealing outfits while they served coffee. Many married men knew better than to get their coffee at one of those places. Some even made sure to get receipts from her to show their wives where they got their coffee that day. About twice a year, the city council threatened to shut down those risqué coffee shops, but they never seemed to go away. They just moved from one location to another.

Amanda got her bearings as the man got closer to the counter.

"Good morning! Welcome to Coffee First," she said with a smile.

"I'd like a large coffee with room for cream and a blueberry muffin to go," he said. "Are the muffins good here, Amanda?"

As a reflex, she looked down at her name tag. It always felt odd when strangers knew her name. She then looked at his chest to find his name tag. Two could play this game.

"They are, Lucas Weston. The owner, Mrs. Connelly, makes them fresh every morning." He glanced down at his name tag, too, and she smiled. "That will be $7.32."

He handed her his credit card, and she could feel his eyes on her while she ran it. She looked up and handed him back the card and the receipt.

"Here you go," she said and then turned to pour his coffee and wrap up the muffin.

"Thank you," he said. Then he stepped closer to the counter instead of going over to the side where most people waited under the "Pick Up Orders Here" sign. There was only one other customer in the shop – Timothy, an older man who came every morning to read the newspaper, drink coffee, and eat a cranberry oatmeal muffin.

"So, Amanda, are you from here?" he asked while her back was still turned.

"Yes. I grew up in Spanaway. My parents are teachers," she answered as she walked back to the counter with his coffee and muffin.

"I just moved here six months ago. It's so different from South Carolina. Do you have any ties to the base at all?"

"No, just work close to it. My uncle used to work as a civilian doing office work somewhere out there, but he retired a few years ago."

Lucas looked at his watch, glanced at the door, and then looked back at Amanda.

"I have to be at the office in 10 minutes. We're supposed to fly today. I better get going. It was nice to meet you, Amanda," he said.

"Hope you have a good day," she replied. He started walking to the door and she turned back to start cleaning up from the morning's work. Her shift would be over in two hours, and then she would head to her college classes. Her work shift at Coffee First was from 5 to 11 a.m. Monday through Saturday so she signed up for afternoon and evening classes.

"Amanda, can I have your number?" Amanda heard a voice say as she was washing out the frothing cups. She looked up and saw that Lucas hadn't left the shop yet. She was slightly shocked. She had specifically chosen to work at this coffee shop to avoid being asked out. She really wanted to focus on school and getting her teaching license before getting into any kind of relationship.

"What?" she asked, wanting to make sure she had heard him correctly.

"I would really like to take you out to dinner sometime. Could I have your number, and I'll call you later to figure out details? Please?"

Maybe it was because he was in uniform. Maybe it was because it had never happened before. Or maybe it was because he said please, which made her smile. Amanda didn't really know why she decided to do it, but she grabbed a pen and a small, square napkin and wrote down her number and gave it to him.

"Thank you, Amanda. I'll call you soon," he said, and she watched as he finally walked out the door. As soon as the bell chimed announcing his departure, she smoothed her ponytail and shook her head. She caught Timothy glancing at her with a smile on his face.

"Did you actually give him your number?" Jodie said, putting her arm around Amanda's shoulder.

"How much did you hear?" Amanda asked.

"Enough. I'm proud of you. He was cute," Jodie said. Her short, spiked hair was blue today. It had been green yesterday.

"He probably won't even call. Maybe it was a bet with some pilot," she replied, shaking her head. "Even if he does call, there's no way I'd get serious with anyone in the military. I'm not moving around the country every few years. I've got two years left until I'm done with school and then I can go teach up in Seattle."

"Be careful with making firm plans. Life has a way of keeping us on our toes. Just look at where I am – I was the tomboy who was going to play sports. Now, I do the girly-girl stuff by doing hair and nails at a salon, and I'm a barista for a coffee shop," Jodie said shaking her head. Then, she smiled big. "The thing is, though – I love it!"

"I know. Life may not turn out exactly as planned, but I can at least make sure I get my teaching degree, and I can make sure I don't fall in love with anyone in the military."

The bell chimed, and a group of eight people walked in for what looked like a breakfast meeting. Amanda and Jodie got back to work. It was busy until the end of Amanda's shift, and she never got her break.

"Let me know if he calls," Jodie said as Amanda got ready to leave for the day. Amanda pulled her phone from her purse and looked. There wasn't even a text from anyone.

"Nothing yet," she said and then she walked out to her car.

CHAPTER THREE

Amanda was studying for finals Tuesday night a few weeks later when her phone rang with a number she didn't recognize. She didn't answer it. If it was important, the person would leave a voicemail. Her friends knew that if they really needed to talk to her, they sometimes had to call twice in a row as she usually didn't pick up the phone on the first ring – either it was in her purse or car or she was studying and couldn't be bothered. This time, she was studying. It was the end of her fall semester of her junior year, and she wanted to keep her grades up so she could have her first pick at a student teaching position. Her first choice was to teach at her alma mater for both nostalgia and convenience. If she was placed in Tacoma, she would have to cut down on her hours at the coffee shop or find a job closer to that school. She was paying her own way through college, although she did have two scholarships that helped cover almost half. She was trying to avoid student loans, but took one out for her first semester to get her started. She hadn't needed any since, and she had already paid

that loan off. She was going where she could afford
– University of Washington Tacoma.

Part of that was because she still lived at home.
Living on campus would have been nice, but college
was much more affordable this way, and her parents
didn't mind at all. She was sure to help around the
house as much as she could. Amanda was an only
child, and her parents were used to her coming and
going and having somewhat separate lives ever since
she could drive. They were both teachers. Her mom
taught third grade, and her father was a high school
science teacher, with a love of chemistry. They had
taught at the next district over in Puyallup, but had
always been able to take and get her from school
since their schedules matched up at some point with
hers.

Amanda was planning to teach high school
English. She loved to read and write. Her favorite
subject in high school was English, and she still kept
in touch with her teachers to talk about books and to
get advice about her college path. It also helped that
most of them were friends with her parents. The
education world seemed small, and even though her
parents taught in a different district, all the area
teachers tended to go to the same conferences every
year in Seattle or Olympia.

The phone buzzed with a voicemail
notification, but Amanda was sure it was a spam
call. She finished reading the section of her book on
Emily Dickinson, jotted down her notes, and then
finally played the voicemail on speaker.

"Hi, Amanda. It's Lucas. I'm sorry it took me
so long to call you. We broke down in Germany and
had to wait for a part to come from Charleston. I'm
back, but only for four days and then they want to
send us on the Hawaii run. Are you free any of the

next three nights? Call me back, and we can set up when and where. Again, sorry for the delay. Hope to talk to you soon. Bye."

Amanda stared at her phone, not really knowing what to think or what to do. She had given up any hope of Lucas calling her after two weeks had gone by. She hadn't thought much about what his job entailed. Being stuck in Germany didn't sound all that bad. Her parents had taken her there before her junior year of high school. It would be interesting to hear more about the kind of life he leads, she thought. One or two dates with him would at least give her something to do after her finals were finished on Thursday. So, Thursday night would work, and if he couldn't do it then, she thought it would be a sign not to go out with him at all. She wouldn't call him back until tomorrow. After all, she waited three weeks to hear from him. He could wait a few hours. She also decided not to even tell Jodie about it until the date actually happened. She would make a bigger deal out of it than Amanda wanted it to be. Maybe Lucas could end up being a good friend – a handsome and tall good friend. She honestly didn't have many friends left in town, as many had gone out of state for college or at least up to Seattle. It wouldn't hurt to have a few more. She saved his contact information in her phone and then got ready for bed. She noticed the smile on her face in the mirror before she brushed her teeth.

"Don't get your hopes up, Amanda," she told herself. "He's in the military and won't be around for long."

CHAPTER FOUR

Before falling asleep, Amanda promised herself she wouldn't call Lucas back until after her shift at Coffee First was done. She almost broke her resolve on the way to work and ended up dialing his number on her break. She stepped out the back door so Jodie wouldn't hear the conversation. She took a deep breath and dialed. It only rang once before he answered it.

"Amanda!"

"Hello," she replied, twisting her hair around her finger with her free hand.

"I'm so glad you called back. I am really sorry we were stuck on our trip for so long. I bet you thought I wasn't going to call."

"I figured you'd forgotten about me."

"There's no way I was forgetting about you. I'm sorry. But, are you free tonight? We could go to dinner somewhere to let me make up for the wait."

"Not tonight. I have my last finals tomorrow. I could go out Thursday night, though."

"Thursday would be great. I don't have to show until Friday afternoon for the next trip."

"Are you gone on trips a lot?"

"I'm out for probably two to three weeks a month. The ops tempo is really high right now."

"Ops tempo?"

"Oh, I'll have to watch the military speak. That's operations tempo – the amount of missions we have to do. Our plane, the C-17, is used for a lot of war support right now."

"Oh, okay. I'd like to hear more about it tomorrow night. Sounds like you live an interesting life."

"It's a job, but we do get to travel to a lot of interesting places. Where do you want to meet tomorrow?"

"Let's go to The Keg in Tacoma on Dock Street. I can meet you there. They have really good food."

"I haven't been there yet. Sounds good. Does 6 p.m. work?"

"That will work great. See you then."

"Sounds good. Thanks for calling back, Amanda. Bye."

"Bye."

Amanda was smiling when she hung up the phone. Jodie looked at her strangely a few times during the rest of the shift, but didn't ask her any questions. Let me see how the date goes, Amanda thought, then I'll tell Jodie all about it.

Amanda replayed the conversation with Lucas in her head as she drove to class that day. After she parked, she shook her head and told herself not to spend too much time thinking about it. It was just going to be a date or two. She needed to focus on the finals she was about to take. She pulled out her notes and reviewed them for a few minutes before getting out of the car. Still, she thought, she hadn't had a date since prom, so she was allowed to be a little excited about it.

Amanda asked her mom look over her outfit before she left Thursday evening. Amanda had picked out black pants and a new teal shirt to wear. She felt confident about how she did on the finals and was sure her grades would come back all As in a few days. Her mom asked her a few questions about Lucas but was very obviously trying to be nonchalant about her daughter going on a date after so long. Her parents had always been very hands-off when it came to Amanda making life choices, but she knew they were there if she wanted their advice. However, they did really encourage her to get her degree before settling down – she remembered them talking to her about going to college as far back as third grade. When Amanda casually mentioned Lucas was in the military, her mom winced. She didn't say it, but Amanda knew she was thinking of the stories they both knew of local girls falling for military men only to be heartbroken when he left or end up divorced after only a few years because they married too soon because he was moving.

"Mom, don't worry. I'm not going to fall for a military guy. His job is on those planes we see flying around, and it sounds interesting. He sounds like he'd be a neat friend."

"Just be careful," her mom said as she tucked a strand of Amanda's straight brown hair behind her ear.

"I will be, Mom. Love you." She grabbed her white jacket as she headed out the door as the temperature was finally dipping into the 50s.

Lucas was waiting outside the restaurant when Amanda arrived. She recognized him from his height more than anything. The khaki pants and green, long-sleeved, button-up shirt still gave off the aura of a military man. His hair was different, though, and not like the military haircut she'd seen at the coffee shop. His blond hair was spiked up a little on the sides instead of flat.

"Good evening," she said as she got closer to the front door.

"Hi, Amanda. You look very nice," he said.

"Thank you."

Lucas looked at his watch and then back to her with a half smile.

"To be honest, I didn't know if you were an on-time person or not, so I got us a reservation for 6:15 p.m. to be safe. We have 15 minutes to kill. Want to hang out at the bar or out here?"

"Let's just sit out here. It's a nice night so far. I heard it's supposed to get down to 45 tonight."

"That's not too bad," he said as they sat down on a bench. "I don't mind the cold at all."

"I love the summer. I don't like being cold," Amanda said. "So, tell me about these trips you take? What do you do on the plane?"

Lucas explained that he was a loadmaster, which meant he was in charge of getting the cargo on and off the plane and making sure it was secured while they were flying. The trips he took could last a few days or a few weeks, depending on the mission. Sometimes they took people, sometimes they took a tank, and sometimes they flew empty. He said he was glad he was able to live in the dorms on base right now because he felt like he was gone more than he was here. He was telling her about getting to visit Neuschwanstein Castle in Germany when he checked his watch again.

"Let me tell you more about the castle when we sit down. Our table should be ready now," Lucas said. He stood up and held out his hand to help her up. She couldn't explain the sensation she felt in her arm when their hands touched. She felt very comfortable with him, and he was very easy to talk with. She looked into his green eyes and smiled. He smiled back and kept her hand in his as they walked into the restaurant and to their table. There was a connection between them already, but Amanda thought that was a bit strange since they barely knew each other.

The next few hours went by quickly as Lucas shared places he'd visited around the world. Amanda was fascinated but shared her own stories of visiting Europe, Alaska, Canada, and Mexico with him, too. Her parents would often rent an RV in the summer, and they would go on long road trips to see anywhere they could drive. The only times she had flown was when they visited Alaska and Europe. They rode in the RV on the way to Alaska to experience the ALCAN highway and went as far as Fairbanks to see Denali, as the locals called Mt. McKinley, but had flown back home to make sure they were back home in time for school. When they went to Europe, they flew into London and left from Rome.

Lucas explained that he had only been to Washington, D.C., for a school trip before joining the Air Force. His parents had divorced when he was 14 but had both stayed in Charleston until he graduated high school. Then, they both wanted to move and told him he was on his own for college unless he wanted to go to Florida where his mom was going to start an art studio or move to Denver where his dad had been hired by a financial firm. Two of his friends were joining the Army, but his grandfather had been in the Air Force, so he decided to go that route. He knew he wanted to do something with planes if he could. His grandfather told wild stories about aircrews during World War II. As a mechanic, he had seen planes in every kind of condition and heard the pilots' stories firsthand on their returns.

When they left the restaurant, Lucas reached for her hand again as they walked across the parking lot to her car.

"I really enjoyed talking with you tonight, Amanda. Can I call you when I get back from this next trip and we can do this again?" He nervously ran his free hand through his hair as he asked and looked at her intently. She wanted to say yes – she could feel a small spark between them. But he was in the military, and she didn't want it to get much bigger. She was strong, though, and could make sure she didn't fall for him. She convinced herself one more date wouldn't hurt anything. They would end up being friends.

"I would love that," she heard herself saying finally, surprised by how true it was. He smiled and then leaned forward and quickly kissed her on the cheek. Then, he opened her car door and let her get in.

"Goodnight, Amanda," he said right before the door closed. She smiled and waved at him before he walked away. She started the car and felt her cheek where he had kissed her. She realized she was in more trouble than she knew. Friends don't kiss each other on the cheek and hold hands. She would go on one more date with him and then she would have to stop. She could not get into a relationship with Lucas – her teaching career, her not wanting to move, and her heart depended on it. She would tell him that, too.

CHAPTER FIVE

"He called you, didn't he?" Jodie asked her during a brief quiet moment between customers. They were offering half-price peppermint mochas that day, which always drew a big crowd.

"What are you talking about?" Amanda asked, trying hard not to smile.

"You've been smiling and humming during the whole morning rush, even to 'Feliz Navidad,' which I know you hate. Did that tall guy finally call you?"

"He did, and we went to dinner last night," Amanda said, smirking at Jodie.

"You kept a secret from me?" Jodie acted. "I'm impressed, girl. How was it? Was he charming? Where did you go?"

"It was great, actually. We met at The Keg. He was really easy to talk with. He's going to call me after he comes back from his next work trip – to Hawaii."

"Man, those military guys have it good. I'd give about anything to be on a beach somewhere."

"Yeah, but that means he's almost never here. No way I could ever get serious with a military guy."

"You can't use the 'serious' word after only one date, girl. You're young, anyway. You have plenty of time to be serious later. Have some fun! It's about time you went out on some dates."

The bell chimed in succession three times, and they got back to work. Amanda hadn't thought about dating Lucas as just being fun. Goodness, she was so serious sometimes, just like her father said. What was the harm in dating someone? He wouldn't be here a lot anyway and then he would move. It could be fun to have a non-serious relationship while finishing up school. Her classes were hardest this year, but would be much easier her senior year. Half of that year was student teaching anyway.

Amanda sighed, feeling herself relax about seeing Lucas as many times as she wanted. As long as she was having fun, it would be okay. Not every relationship had to be serious, and she wasn't looking to get married anytime soon, anyway.

Amanda had almost a month off from school for winter break, and she picked up a second part-time job at a clothing store, Amelie, to save up for her senior year and the summer after graduation. Her current savings would cover this next semester and about half of her senior fall semester. Amanda truly enjoyed her job at the coffee shop, but really looked forward to the job at Amelie because her best friend would be working there with her. Juliana would be home from MIT, and they were usually able to get the same shifts. Amanda would start at Amelie Saturday, but Juliana wouldn't be in town until Sunday night and she wouldn't see her until work Monday afternoon. They had plans to go out to dinner together after work and get all caught up – especially since Amanda hadn't mentioned Lucas to Juliana yet.

Juliana let her brown curls out of her ponytail as they were walking out of Amelie. It had been a fairly quiet shift, mainly sorting through the weekend's returns and organizing all the stacks of clothes that had been toppled over by shoppers looking for a certain size. They chatted occasionally when they were near each other about classes but nothing super personal. They never did that at the store in case their supervisor walked by. Beatrice was known to dismiss workers very easily if she didn't like how they were working, and that included socializing on the job.

"Any new, good restaurants open this fall?" she asked Amanda as they walked to their cars.

"There's a new wing place in the mall, and we finally got a Sonic out in Puyallup," Amanda replied.

"I think I feel like Greek. Want to go to Phyllos?"

"I could have bet $1,000 you were going to ask to go there. Of course. You know I'm always willing to eat a gyro."

"Sounds good. See you there in 10."

After they ordered, Amanda told Juliana all about Lucas – from the coffee shop to the phone call and the date. Juliana listened, wide-eyed, until Amanda finished.

"You got picked up at work and went out with a military guy?" Juliana asked when Amanda was finished. "Are you the same Amanda Schaffer I said goodbye to in August?"

They both laughed and then Juliana asked if she'd get to meet him.

"Why not? Although, I do have to wait for him to get back from Hawaii. I think he is scheduled to get back tonight, but their missions often get delayed, he said."

"Missions? Don't start talking like a military person now. Ugh, do you remember Jason? You had told me not to date a military guy, and I should have listened to you."

Juliana had dated Jason a few times the summer after they graduated high school and then she found out he had a girlfriend back home the hard way. The girlfriend had decided to make a surprise visit when Juliana was watching a movie at Jason's apartment. Luckily, the girlfriend was so mad at Jason that Juliana just slipped out the door and never looked back.

"It's just for fun, anyway. He seems like he could be an interesting friend," Amanda said.

"Friend, huh? Didn't you say he held your hand? I don't think he has friends in mind," Juliana replied.

"Well, I do. And it's only been one date so far. There won't be a ring on this finger for a long time."

"Let me know when he does call, and maybe I can organize a small party you could invite him to. There's always plenty of people who want to get away from their families for a bit while home on break."

"That sounds like a great idea. Now, tell me about all the guys you dated this semester."

Juliana was a structural engineer major, and there were 10 guys for every girl in most of her classes at MIT. Juliana always had a lot of friends around her, while Amanda had just a few close friends – they were very much opposites. Their friendship went back to the third grade when they bonded over both having a missing sack lunch on a field trip to an art museum. Mrs. Frindlay had felt bad for them and bought them Wendy's from across the street, but she made them come with her and eat it at the restaurant so none of the other kids would be jealous. They were sworn to secrecy and started hanging out with each other at recess after that. They only lived six blocks from each other, so as soon as their parents would let them, they walked to each other's house almost every day. Amanda knew Juliana would be key to helping her keep her relationship – if that's what it turned out to be – with Lucas in check.

When Amanda checked her phone on her way to Amelie after working at Coffee First the next day, there was a voicemail from Lucas. She smiled as she played it on speaker while she drove.

"Hello, Amanda. It's Lucas. We just got back after we maxed our crew day. Shorty, one of the pilots, wanted to be back for his wife's ultrasound appointment. I've been awake for 20 hours now. That means I'm tired, and I can't wait to get to my bed and sleep. But I want to talk with you, too, so give me a call anytime. If I don't answer, it's only because I'm asleep and I'll call you back when I wake up if it's a decent hour. Hope your week's been good so far. Bye."

The call had been made about three hours earlier. She decided to wait until after work at Amelie to call him back so he could get some sleep. When she did call, it went to voicemail after a few rings and just as she was about to leave him a message, her phone started ringing. He was calling her back. She switched to his call.

"Hello," she said. "Welcome back to Washington."

"Thanks," he replied and yawned. "I'm just glad I was finally able to get some sleep."

"Did I wake you up? You can call me back later or tomorrow."

"I was actually starting to wake up a little. I was getting hungry. It usually takes me two days after a trip to get back in the right time zone."

"Jet lag all the time – that probably wouldn't be the best recruitment slogan."

Lucas laughed, and Amanda found herself laughing, too.

"That's a good one. I'll have to tell the guys at work that one."

There was a pause.

"So, they want us to leave again on Friday," Lucas said. "And it's to the sandbox, I mean, Afghanistan, so I will probably be gone for two weeks. They picked us single guys to do the Christmas and New Year's missions."

"Oh, did you have plans for Christmas?"

"Nothing set in stone because I thought they might do this, but I haven't been with either of my parents for Christmas in two years so I was thinking of visiting them both if I got time off. I'll have to do it sometime not around the holidays next year instead."

"Sorry about that."

"It is what it is, I guess. Hey, can we meet up this week sometime, though? My buddy told me about a great seafood restaurant up in Seattle that we could go to if you don't mind the drive. Would tomorrow night work?"

"Tomorrow night would work. I get off at Amelie around 4 on Wednesdays. I just can't be out too late as I have to be at Coffee First at 5 in the morning."

"Can I pick you up around 5?"

"Sure. That will work." She gave him her parents' address. She had told him all about her college financial situation on their first date and he thought she was being really smart. He said he would eventually go to college, too, and that it was nice to not have to face a mountain of debt for it since the military would pay for it.

"Well, at least our side is moving a little. The cars going south are at a standstill," Amanda said quietly. As soon as they had passed one of the last Tacoma exits, the traffic on I-5 North had slowed to a crawl. They had only moved two miles in 20 minutes, and Amanda could see Lucas was worried and upset. They hadn't spoken much in those 20 minutes, and Lucas mostly stared straight ahead. When she spoke up, it was like he was shaken out of a zone – like he had almost forgotten she was there. His hands moved from the top to the sides of the steering wheel, and he sat back in his seat and sighed.

"We're never going to make it in time for our reservation. I don't think it's the type of restaurant that would hold it."

"We're going to Elliott's, right?"

"Yes," he said. "I forget you know this area really well. I'm used to hanging around military people who don't know anything about where they're living."

"Elliott's won't hold the reservation, and they are always booked up. Sorry, but we probably need to change our plans. Do you like BBQ?"

"I do, but I did get spoiled on authentic BBQ when I was in Oklahoma. Is there a good place near here?"

"There is – Saucey's near the airport. We just need to get to the airport exit in about 10 miles. They have some really cool celebrity photos on the walls there. The owner is from Mississippi. It's the best BBQ you'll get around here."

"I'm game if you are. Sorry, I did want to take you somewhere nice."

"It's okay. I'm pretty easygoing about things. I'm more used to a BBQ place than Elliott's anyway. I wasn't poor growing up, but two teachers' salaries didn't make us a rich family either."

"I hear you. We only went to fancy places for my father's work Christmas party. I never liked wearing a suit. I don't think my dad did either, but Mom liked to dress up, and dinner and drinks were free for them that evening. There was usually a children's buffet and movies and crafts for us to do. I stopped going once I was 12 and they could leave me home alone."

"There's the exit," Amanda interrupted him. "It'll be off to the right about two blocks down."

Another night went by quickly for Amanda. He shared some stories from his Hawaii trip and gave her a lei he had bought there. She shared about the old lady she followed around Amelie who would pick up and item, walk a few steps, put it down on another shelf, and pick up another item. She did it for an hour and then left the store without buying anything. Lucas got her home before 10, and her parents were still out for their Thursday night bowling league. He walked her to the door, holding her hand again.

"I guess I won't see you again until next year," Lucas said. "I'll call you when we get back, if that's okay with you."

"I'll be looking forward to it," Amanda replied. She felt at ease in his company and realized she would miss him over the next two weeks.

"If we stop in Germany on the way home, I'll bring you back some German chocolate. That alone should be worth going out with me again. I'll let you pick the restaurant next time – you're much better at it than I am."

Before she could respond, he leaned in for a quick kiss. As he pulled away, she found herself smiling.

"Be safe, Lucas," she said as he turned to go back to his car.

"I will, Amanda," he replied. "See you soon!"

CHAPTER SIX

In the 16 days while Lucas was gone, Amanda stayed busy with work and seeing friends who were in town for the winter break. She started reading ahead for some of her classes and updated her resume for when she would apply for a student teaching position in the fall. Christmas had been quiet with just her parents, but Juliana had thrown a huge New Year's Eve party like she had since they were 16. Amanda enjoyed it more than usual as she found herself being able to talk to the guys without feeling any pressure of Juliana trying to match her up with anyone. Instead of trying to find some random person to kiss at midnight, she just closed her eyes and remembered Lucas' kiss.

Lucas wasn't back by the time Juliana left for MIT, so she didn't get to meet him.

"You'll meet him this summer if he's still around," Amanda said as she helped Juliana pack up her car on her break between the Coffee First shift and her Amelie shift. Juliana usually came back home for spring break but was headed to Mexico for spring break that year – a present from her parents. "I promise I'll keep you updated."

"You better. Remember your daily mantra – 'This is all for fun. I will not fall for a military guy.'"

"This is all for fun. I will not fall for a military guy," Amanda repeated and laughed. "Drive safe!"

Amanda was driving back from work when Lucas called the next day. She could tell he was tired right away.

"I just got back to my dorm room," he said. "That was a long trip. How are you doing?"

"I'm good. Just one more week until classes start again."

"Man, I missed just about all of your break. You wouldn't happen to have any days off this week?"

"Just Sunday. My last day at Amelie is Friday, but I have to work at Coffee First Saturday morning."

"I was thinking, if you were willing, you could give me a non-touristy tour of the area on Sunday. But I don't want to wait that long to see you. Can we do dinner one night, too? I was able to pick up some German chocolate."

"Sunday sounds good. I just have to be back by 6 to have dinner with my parents. We have a tradition of celebrating the night before school starts. It's a teacher thing. We could do dinner on Wednesday again. I still get off at Amelie at 4 on Wednesdays."

"Remember, though, you have to pick the," he paused to yawn, "restaurant."

"We'll visit one of my favorites," she replied. "Now, get some rest."

"Okay. See you Wednesday night."

After Lucas picked her up, Amanda gave him directions to her and Juliana's favorite place, Phyllos. She didn't tell him it was Greek food, wanting to see his reaction when they pulled up.

"Is this Greek?" he asked.

"Yep, it's one of my favorite restaurants. My friend Juliana and I ate here at least once a week in high school."

"I love Greek food!" he said.

As they went into the restaurant, Amanda was greeted by name by the hostess, Elana, who only offered a menu to Lucas.

"You'll be having the regular, right, Amanda?" Elena asked.

"Yes, please," she answered.

"You really do come here often," Lucas commented. "What do you usually get?"

"The lamb gyro is my favorite, and it comes with a Greek side salad. Everything is good here, though."

Lucas decided on the chicken gyro, and they planned to split an order of baklava for dessert. They got caught up on the past two weeks, and the conversation flowed easily between them.

It wasn't until they got back into the car that he gave her the German chocolates – six different kinds of candy bars. She opened one right there for them to share, and they sat in the car almost another hour talking until they both started yawning.

"I better get you back so you can get some sleep before work," he said. "I have to head back into the office tomorrow, too. They're having a commander's call."

"What is that?"

"It's a mass briefing," he said. She must have looked confused because he started to clarify his answer. "Our squadron commander will have all of us who work for him gather in the big conference room and he'll talk to us about how the squadron is doing, upcoming activities, and any news about our career field. They're usually pretty boring."

"Well, I hope for your sake it's somewhat interesting."

When they pulled up to Amanda's house, he walked her to the door again. Just before they reached the front step, her parents pulled into the driveway where the garage was on the side of the house.

"Would you want to meet my parents?" she offered, hoping he would say no.

"I would love to," he replied, so she opened up the front door and they went inside.

"Mom and Dad, this is Lucas," Amanda said. "Lucas, this is my mom, Veronica, and my dad, Charles."

"Nice to meet you, Mr. And Mrs. Schaffer," Lucas said and reached out to shake her dad's hand.

"Where are you from, Lucas?"

"I grew up in South Carolina – Charleston," he replied. "I've been living here for almost a year now."

"Charleston is such a nice city," her mom said. "We went there on our honeymoon. It was our first RV trip."

Amanda yawned and sighed.

"Oh, sorry," she said as they all looked at her. "I must be tired."

"I should go then," Lucas said. "It was really nice to meet you."

"You, too," her mom said. Amanda walked him to the door and stepped outside. Lucas gave her a quick kiss and then said goodnight.

"See you Sunday," he said as she walked back into the house.

"Well, he seems nice," her mother said as she picked up their bowling shoes to put in the hall closet. Her father was right behind her with their bowling ball bags.

"He is. Do you want to try some of the German chocolate he brought me back from his trip?" Amanda asked.

"Yes, please. He was in Germany?" her dad asked.

"He travels all over in a military plane – something 17," she replied.

"That's interesting," her mother said. "Let me know if we should have him over for dinner sometime."

"Oh, it's nothing serious like that at all. It's just fun to have someone to go out to dinner with," she replied.

"Okay," her mother said, sounding like she was unconvinced. "Well, I think it's time for me to turn in. Coming, Charles?"

"Right behind you, Roni," her dad said.

Amanda sighed. She realized she wasn't very convincing the way she was talking about Lucas. She headed up to bed herself but was thinking about all the places she wanted to show Lucas on Sunday. He had been so busy going on trips, he had hardly seen any of the tourist spots in the area. She decided they would start with the Puyallup Fairgrounds and end at Mt. Rainier.

Amanda was about to head out to door to pick up Lucas at Coffee First on Sunday when her phone rang. It was Lucas.

"Good morning," she said. "I'm just about to head your way."

"I'm glad I caught you before you left. I have bad news. I got a call last night that I have to go up today for some requals. Something about an inspection coming next month before we ... well, it's a big hassle, but I can't go out today. I'm sorry."

"It's okay," she said, trying to hide her disappointment. "What's a requal?"

"Oh, we have to be qualified to do certain things in the aircraft every quarter, and I'm missing a few. They normally schedule the flights a few days out but they're wanting these to get done quickly. Our files are going to get checked in a few weeks," he explained.

"Sounds complicated," she said. "We could always do it another Sunday."

"True," he sighed. "They're also talking about sending me on the road again this week. I would probably leave really early on Wednesday. It's a Pacific trip, so I'll be gone for at least a week."

It was Amanda's turn to sigh. That only left Monday night to see Lucas, and that was when the Future Teachers Association met at the school and they were starting to really get into how to navigate the student teaching job applications. She told him she couldn't miss the meeting.

"I guess I'll see you when you get back then." She knew she wasn't doing a good job of hiding the disappointment in her voice.

"Could I start emailing you while I'm on the road?" he asked. "It gets really expensive to call from overseas, but I could take my laptop and email you with the hotel WiFi."

"That would be nice," Amanda said. They swapped email addresses, and she wished him safe flights.

"If you see a big, gray plane flying around the area around noon today, that'll be me."

"I'll wave," she said.

She spent the morning doing homework and decided to go to the library for research in the afternoon. On her way to the library, she did see a military plane flying, so she waved and smiled. It was nice that he wanted to email her and stay in touch instead of going another week or two without talking.

When she checked her email Monday morning before heading to work, she had a short email from him saying hi and wanting to make sure he had the right email. He wished her a good day. She sent a quick reply back just to let him know he did have the right email address.

Amanda was surprised to see two cars in the parking lot when she got to Coffee First Wednesday morning. One was Jodie's red VW Beetle. The other one looked like Lucas' blue car. As she parked, she saw him emerge from the blue car.

"Good morning, Amanda," he said. "I don't have to report until 5:30, so I thought I should bring the crew some coffee and muffins."

"Well, we don't open until 5:30, but maybe I could help you out," she said. "If you ask nicely."

"Actually, if I don't get the coffee, I'm fine. I really just wanted to see you before I left," he reached out and grabbed her hand before she started to unlock the back door and pulled her closer. He kissed her before she could even think about what was happening. She smiled at him after he stepped back and turned to unlock the door.

"Okay, I guess you asked nicely. How many coffees would you need?"

Jodie helped her make the coffees and wrap up the muffins for Lucas. She asked him a lot of questions, and both Lucas and Amanda knew she was grilling him for Amanda's sake. Jodie was smiling at the end and sent Amanda to help him take the items to his car.

"I'll send you an email when we land in Japan," he said after they set everything in his car. She let him give her one more quick kiss before he got in his car and left.

She could tell Jodie was trying hard to not say anything when she went back into the shop. They quietly got everything set up, and as Amanda went to unlock the front door and turn on the "Open" sign, Jodie finally spoke up.

"Amanda, that boy is really into you," she said.

"What?"

"I'm saying if you don't want to get serious, you better be careful. He already looks like he has eyes only for you."

"He's fun to hang out with when he's in town," Amanda said, shaking her head at Jodie. "There's no getting serious with someone who's not here half of the time."

"We'll see," Jodie said and then door chimed.

CHAPTER SEVEN

When Lucas got back in town nine days later, they went out to dinner at a new Mexican place Amanda wanted to try, Los Amigos. It was nice not to feel the need to get completely caught up about the last week since they were able to email a few times while he was gone. For Amanda, the start of the conversation felt less awkward than it ever had. After they got caught up, they talked more about their childhoods and families.

Lucas explained why his parents divorced. His parents had always acted civil toward each other, but they had grown apart. They had both met people through work and ended up having affairs at the same time. They didn't get emotional – at least not in front of him – and they let him choose who he would live with permanently. They didn't want him moving his things back and forth all the time, but he would be welcome at either home any time. His father kept the house, and his mother moved into an apartment downtown to be closer to the art studio where she worked. He decided to stay with his dad at his house, but made sure to visit his mom at least twice a week. It actually worked rather well, and his parents were able to spend time together with him when he wanted, which was mainly on his birthday and some holidays.

Amanda told him about Juliana – how they met and how even though they were opposites in a lot of ways, they always remained good friends. They shared worst date stories and found out they both only dated two people in high school.

After they ordered dessert, Lucas got quiet and started staring at the back wall. She wasn't sure if she should say anything, so after a minute or two of silence, she excused herself to go to the bathroom. When she came back, the fried ice cream with two spoons was at the table. Lucas looked at her when she sat down but with a serious look on his face.

"I have to tell you something, Amanda," he said. "I kept waiting for the right time to bring it up, but it'll never be the right time. I found out at the commander's call I have to leave next month for a six-month deployment to Qatar."

Amanda moved the spoon that was almost to her mouth back to the bowl.

"You'll be gone for six months? To where? That's a really, really long time."

"I know. I'm sorry. Qatar is in the Middle East. I'll show you on a map later if you want," Lucas hesitated and then spoke up again.

"I didn't think it would be an option for our squadron for another year or two, so I hadn't brought it up yet. I'm sorry."

"I hadn't even realized you could deploy," she said. "I was just getting used to you being gone for your trips."

Amanda took two bites of the ice cream while she let it sink in that he would be deploying. He reached for her hand after she put the spoon down.

"Amanda, I know we haven't known each other very long, so I can't ask you to not date anyone else while I'm gone. But can we stay in touch and just see where things go?"

"I'm not sure. Can I think about it?"

"I think that's the best I can hope for right now," Lucas said. He gently squeezed her hand and then let it go.

"I'm done," she said.

"Me, too," Lucas replied. "I should probably get you home."

They met up twice more for dinner and then finally had the tour of Tacoma on Sunday, Feb. 14. He was scheduled to leave three days later. They acted more like friends on those dates, though. Lucas didn't try to kiss her and she was glad. She knew she was going to miss his company while he was deployed, but didn't want to feel more attached than she already was. For the tour date, she picked him up in the parking lot right outside the base, and they visited the art museum and glass museum in downtown Tacoma and had lunch at a little deli nearby. They spent the afternoon visiting Mt. Rainier National Park and had a picnic dinner. When they got back to Lucas' car outside the base gate, he asked her to wait for a minute – he had something for her.

He brought over a small bonsai plant and six envelopes.

"I packed up all of my things, but I didn't want to throw away this plant. I bought it when I first moved here to have something green in my room. Will you take care of it for me?"

"Sure," she said, taking the plant and looking at the Oriental designs on the planter. She put in on the passenger seat in her car.

"I also wrote you some letters — one for each month I'm gone. It's nothing big, but just in case the Internet isn't working well and I can't email, you'll have something from me."

Amanda took the letters from him and then gave him a big hug.

"Take care of yourself, Lucas," she said. "I'll email you."

"You, too, Amanda," he kissed the top of her head and then let her go. "I'm going to miss you."

Then he walked back to his car and she got into hers. She drove away first, looking back in her rearview mirror just once to see he hadn't moved yet. He was watching her drive away. She would miss him, but she was trying really hard to just think of him as a friend now. She'd go back to her life of school and work, just with an added pen pal.

"He's just a friend," she said out loud. "He's just a friend." A few tears fell down her cheeks as she repeated it a few more times on her way home.

CHAPTER EIGHT

The envelopes Lucas had given Amanda were marked with each month he would be gone from March to August. Lucas was scheduled to return August 15, just two weeks before the start of her senior year. When she called Juliana a few hours after saying goodbye to Lucas, Juliana told her it was the perfect time to date a few other guys now that she remembered how fun dating could be. Jodie was more sympathetic as she saw day after day how Amanda's mood was affected by Lucas' leaving. It was almost a week before Amanda got an email from him. By that time, she was ahead on her schoolwork and starting a research paper that wasn't due until early May.

His email told about their long travels to Qatar and described where he would be living for 6 months. It was a large, metal rectangular container that he would share with three other loadmasters. There were two bunk beds at either end and each wall had two desks and two lockers alongside it. He had a bottom bunk, a locker, and his own small desk. The Internet was spotty, but better in the early morning when most people were working out or heading to work. He said a few other guys were going to train for a half marathon while they were there and he might join them. They would run in the evenings. His training would be spotty as they would be flying at least a few times a week, but there were two others in the group who had schedules like his and they could adapt the training plan together. He was actually leaving in three days for his first mission. He couldn't tell her where, though. He asked her about classes and work and how his bonsai plant was doing. He signed off by writing "Missing you, Lucas."

She wrote him back right away and then didn't hear from him until after she opened her first letter.

> Amanda,
>
> I'm glad you accepted these monthly letters. Maybe I'm being selfish wanting you to think of me at least once a month while I'm gone, even though we decided to just be friends (for now). I guess you'll actually think of me more often if you agree to take care of my plant.
>
> I thought I would just share a story with you.
>
> I went to my first air show with my neighbor, Daren, when I was 10. His father worked on the local military base and had overheard Daren and I talking about how I'd never been on the base. We spent the whole day there and went in every airplane that was open. My favorite was the helicopters, though. I collected every free postcard or poster that was being handed out and pinned them on my bedroom wall as soon as we got

home. Before then, I just thought about either being a professional baseball player or a businessman like my dad when I grew up. That night, I thought about being a pilot and spending my life traveling the world. I went to the air show every year after that and asked a lot of questions to any pilot who would talk to me. Why didn't I end up becoming a pilot? Well, that's a story for another letter.

Lucas

Amanda hadn't followed the news much until Lucas deployed and then she checked it every morning and night, looking for any article about military in the Middle East. There weren't many on a daily basis, and the first one she came across was about two soldiers who had died after driving across an IED. She was worried and emailed him to see how safe he was while he was over there. It was three days before his reply came through.

He told her she shouldn't worry much at all. They didn't drive around but only left the base if they were in the airplane. It was almost as if he was confined to the base there in Washington and could only leave if they went on a mission. He talked about the gym, the chow hall, and the exchange, which was like a small store filled with snacks, books, movies, magazines, and little trinkets. They took cash, but no coins. Instead they had cardboard disks that were used as coins. He attached a few pictures of the "money" in the email and promised to save a few for her to see when he got home. She felt better after reading the email but still found herself worrying about him every now and again.

April's letter told her that he wanted to take flying lessons in high school, but he couldn't afford it and his parents didn't really want him to do it as they thought it was too dangerous. When it came time to decide what to do after high school, he thought the military would at least get him close to the planes. He would try to start working on his degree after this deployment and could always apply to become an officer and a pilot as long as he did it before he turned 30. He wasn't sure yet, though. He really liked his job, and he would have to get a degree first. Time would tell, he ended.

In the midst of getting ready for the end-of-semester finals and finishing up her research paper, Amanda forgot about May's letter until a few days into May. Lucas had been on trips a lot, so she only got an email from him about once a week. She was getting better about not thinking about him all the time and thought she was finally convinced to think of him only as a friend. She was starting to look for a summer job, too. Amelie had changed managers, and they were no longer willing to hire as many short-term employees. She had an interview with a tutoring company in Olympia in a few days, which would look good on her resume. She would have to fill out all her applications for student teaching jobs the first week of classes in August.

Amanda,

I have a confession to make. The day I asked for your number was not the first time I saw you. I had come into Coffee First a few weeks earlier with a crew before we headed on a trip. I hadn't known they were planning on stopping for coffee before we left, so I had already grabbed a thermos from my dorm for the trip. I hung back while they ordered. Before fixing their drinks, you took a coffee and muffin over to an older gentleman sitting with a newspaper. He reminded me of my Grandpa. The way you smiled and greeted him caught my eye. I could tell you were a decent person who actually cared about this older customer sitting in a coffee shop, even though you were young. (Okay, I know you're my age, but we are young.) After all the training I had gone through during the summer and fall, it was nice to see someone being nice to someone else. You kept coming to my mind while we were on that trip, so I knew I would have to stop back and see you. It took me a while to get up the courage, but I'm glad I did.

Lucas

She called Juliana right away after reading that letter. He was definitely not thinking about keeping their relationship as just friends. She would really have to decide when he got back if she would want to keep things on the friendship level or let it become a real relationship. She really didn't know what she wanted to do, but he was slowly becoming a part of her life. Juliana gave her a pep talk and promised to set her up with a few guys as soon as she was home for the summer. For the first time ever, Amanda agreed to let Juliana arrange a few dates for her as long as they were double dates.

They were getting ready for the first double date at Amanda's house a few weeks later when

Juliana saw June's letter from Lucas sitting on her desk.

"June is only a few days away. Let's open it now."

"I'd really rather wait," Amanda said, but Juliana was already sitting on her bed, opening up the letter. There was really no harm in reading it now, Amanda thought, so she put her eye shadow down on her desk and sat down next to her friend.

Amanda,

Welcome to summer! I looked up when and where the state fair is there in Washington. I saw it wasn't until August, but that it happens right near us in Puyallup. I should be home in time to go. Have you been? I know it seems like a silly question, but I know people often don't go to events near them. I went to the state fair every year in Columbia. It was about two hours away, and my mom would wake me up early and we would get there when it opened and spend the whole day eating fair food, riding rides, and looking at all the exhibits.

When I was in high school, I was able to enter some of my woodworking projects through FFA. Yep, I can make things out of wood. My only project to get a ribbon was a yard game of Connect Four. I got third place, but won $50. I had to sell my equipment before I went to basic training since my parents were moving and it wasn't worth putting in storage. Hopefully I can move out of the dorms shortly after the deployment and get an apartment and start

making some things again. Maybe I can
make something for you.

Lucas

When Juliana finished reading, she looked up at
Amanda and found her smiling.

"He's one of those 4H fair geeks," Juliana said.
"Perfect for you – they're always those nice, polite
guys who hold open doors."

"I had no idea he did that," Amanda said.

"At least this one wasn't too sappy. Let's go see
if you can get your mind off him for a few hours.
Thomas is quite charming. Although Matt is better
looking, so he's mine." Juliana had met the two boys
at a party the weekend before. Amanda was sure
they would both focus their attention on Juliana, but
Juliana really wanted to help Amanda out, so she
was willing to play along.

They went to Phyllos and then to a movie, and
while Amanda had fun, she could clearly see both
guys were vying for Juliana's attention and being
extra nice and polite to her to make an impression
on Juliana.

Lucas' July and August letters told her about his
childhood pets – a dog named Sally who loved to eat
socks and a cat named Prince who loved to eat dog
food. They were originally his parents' pets but kept
him company growing up. They died within the
same year when he was 11, and his parents didn't
want to get any pets after that. Both letters were
filled with stories of the pets and how he wanted to
get a dog one day and thought an Australian
Shepherd was the smartest dog and the one he
wanted to get.

Juliana didn't bring up going out on another date until about two weeks before Lucas came home. Juliana convinced Amanda to go out to an Irish festival with Anthony by herself. Even Juliana had admitted after the double date that it didn't work if they were interested in her. Anthony worked with Juliana at the country club that summer, and he was a "nice guy, just like Lucas," according to Juliana. He went to college across the state in Spokane.

Anthony picked her up in a small, red pickup truck. He was tall and skinny and had long, wavy blond hair. Her parents were out that night. Anthony opened the truck door for her, and they made small talk on the ride to downtown Tacoma. He seemed very quiet until they couldn't find a parking spot for his truck. His frustration level rose quickly, and he didn't want to listen when Amanda offered to give him directions to a parking lot she knew of a few blocks away that only charged $8 an hour. Instead, they drove around for 25 minutes with him muttering under his breath until he found a spot on a street that was free. He then took a deep breath, turned to Amanda, and said, "Let's go enjoy this thing."

Amanda tried to enjoy the music and looking at some of the booths, but it felt awkward. They got some meat pasties for dinner, and they couldn't find much to talk about while they ate. Amanda decided to end the date early and told him she was starting to get a headache and wanted to go home. The ride home was quiet except for the country songs on the radio. He walked her to the door and while he said he had a nice time and would like to see her again, she knew it wasn't true. She called Juliana after she got settled and told her all about the night.

"Well, I guess you might as well keep dating Lucas. You might have to just deal with the military thing," Juliana said. "But I do need to meet him. I don't have to leave until August 20, so if he gets back on time, you have to let me see him."

Amanda laughed and realized Juliana was right. She was going to have to deal with the military thing. She also knew she was probably going to still date Lucas – if he wanted to, although she was fairly certain that's what he was hoping for all along.

CHAPTER NINE

L ucas had emailed her specific instructions about how to meet him when he came back from his deployment. Her name would be on a list at the gate, and she would need to show her driver's license to the gate guard. He gave her step-by-step directions on how to get to the base operations building where they would arrive. He told her if she couldn't come or didn't want to, it was okay with him, but he at least wanted to meet up sometime soon after he got back.

Amanda thought he should have someone to greet him when he got back after serving his country on a deployment for six months, so she took the day off of work and made her way to the base on August 15. There was a big crowd inside the Base Terminal, and Amanda felt out of place with all the spouses and children in the crowd. There were a few people in uniform milling around. Amanda kept herself busy by looking at the artwork on the walls of older military aircraft.

"May I have your attention? The deployed military members of the 7th Airlift Squadron have landed. They should start coming through the terminal in about 20 minutes. It may take an hour for everyone to come through as they have to process through customs and find their luggage. Thank you for supporting all of them while they served their country. Your sacrifices here back at home are appreciated. Thank you."

Amanda went over to line the hallways with the rest of the crowd. A woman with short, black hair and a toddler in her arms whose head was lying on her shoulder, stood next to Amanda.

"Hi, I'm Terri," she said. "I don't think I've seen you before at any of the squadron events. Who are you waiting for?"

"I'm waiting for Lucas Weston. He's a friend of mine."

"He's flown with my husband, Will, a few times," Terri said. "How did you meet Lucas?"

"We met at the coffee shop I work at – Coffee First."

"I'm so glad you didn't say one of those bikini coffee shops. I was so shocked when I found out about those up here. Are you from here? What's your name?"

"I'm Amanda, and I grew up in Tacoma."

Before she could say anything else, the first man came through the doors at the end of the hallway, and a little girl ran down the hall shouting, "Daddy!" Amanda smiled and noticed all the conversations died down as people started watching the doors for their loved ones. Lucas was about the 15th person to come through the doors. Amanda just stepped toward the middle of the hallway as he walked toward her with a big smile on his face and a huge tan duffel bag hiked over his shoulder. She returned the smile, and they walked together toward the exit. Lucas opened the door for her, and after she walked through, he offered her his hand. She took it, and he pulled her in for a kiss. She let herself fall into the moment, and as they finally pulled away, she realized he was definitely more than just a friend.

CHAPTER TEN

Amanda and Lucas' first date after he got back was to the state fair — with Juliana. They ended up spending the whole day there. Lucas made sure they found the 4-H and FFA buildings, and they spent almost an hour looking at the projects kids had done. Lucas was impressed by some of the wooden dressers made by FFA kids. He said he'd have to try making one of those one day. Juliana seemed to get along with him great, and Amanda was relieved that Lucas wasn't flirting with Juliana. He was treating Juliana like a friend, not a potential date. Juliana grabbed a picture of Amanda and Lucas at the top of the Ferris wheel. Juliana spent a lot of time raving about how nice he was when they chatted on the phone later that night.

"I approve, Amanda. He seems good for you," she said. "See where it goes."

"If he still wants to date, I think I'd be up for it. I just still don't know about the whole military thing if this ever gets serious."

"I guess you can deal with that if it comes, but at least he doesn't seem like the typical military guy. He seems more like just a normal guy."

"True, but he will have to move one day. They can't stay in one place forever. I don't know if I'd ever be able to leave Washington."

"Well, that's a while off anyway. Maybe you'll just date him while he's here and then you'll find someone even better."

"Maybe," Amanda replied. She couldn't think of anyone being much better than Lucas.

Lucas called shortly after she got off the phone with Juliana. He had gotten a call from a coworker about looking at an apartment that night, and they had gotten back from the fair just in time for him to get to the apartment.

"How'd it go?" she asked.

"It was a really small space, but it did have two bedrooms. We're going to look at two more places tomorrow before we decide."

"That's smart. I can't wait to get my own place next year."

"So, I heard Juliana say she was leaving the day after tomorrow. We can hold off on going out to dinner until she leaves if you want to spend time with her."

"Oh, I'm going to spend all day with her helping her pack and load up her car. She may be smart, but she always overpacks and has trouble fitting everything back into her car. Then she'll spend the evening with her family. I'm free tomorrow night – unless you were looking for a way out of our date?"

"Nope. Just trying to be nice. I can't wait to have all your attention just for myself." The line went quiet for a few. "I missed you, Amanda. A lot."

"I missed you, too, Lucas. I'm looking forward to dinner tomorrow, too."

They went to The Keg again and got a booth by the window that overlooked the water. Lucas was fairly quiet until after they ordered.

"So, Amanda, I think we should talk," he said, "about us."

Amanda looked at him and put her hand through her hair. When she put it back down on the table, he put his hand on hers.

"I know we've only known each other a short amount of time and have only been out on a handful of dates compared to that time, but I would really like to give this thing a shot and see where it goes. I don't want to assume what you're thinking and feeling about me, though. So, I want to ask ..."

Amanda had grabbed her water glass to stall and after taking a few sips had begun to put it down and it slipped – water went everywhere, but mostly toward Lucas.

"I'm so sorry," Amanda said quietly and started sopping up the mess with her napkin. Lucas put his napkin to stop the water from flowing off the table, stood up, and then motioned for Amanda to scoot over on her booth seat. She did, and he sat down and turned toward her.

"It's just water, and it will clean up easily," he said. "Now, before I lose my nerve. Amanda, I like you, and I think we should date exclusively. I want to see where this goes."

She looked at him and then down at her hands for a minute before looking back at him to answer.

"I like you, too, Lucas. I would like to see where this goes, too. But, I have to be honest. I don't like the fact that you're in the military. Nothing against the military, but more against knowing you'll be moving away at some point."

"That's understandable," he said and turned back toward the spill and started cleaning it up a little more. Their waitress came over to check on them and saw the mess and brought over more napkins. The booth behind them was empty, so she asked them to move to that booth. Lucas sat down on one side and this time, Amanda motioned for him to scoot down and she sat down next to him.

"But, despite that, I'd like to see where this goes, too," she said. Then, she leaned over and kissed him – the first time she had initiated a kiss. Lucas smiled and then kissed her again.

Amanda tried to give the bonsai plant back to Lucas, but he asked if she would hang on to it. He had read a book on minimalism during the deployment and had realized with all his traveling, he really didn't need many things. He and his coworker had decided on the small apartment to save money. Most of the time only one of them would be home anyway. Lucas explained that they could actually make a little money each month since the government gave them an allowance for housing and it was more than their rent and utilities. Amanda saw it for the first time when she went to their "New Apartment Party." It was a two-bedroom apartment located on the second floor of a three-story building. There was a locked front door for their stairwell with an intercom buzzer system to let people in. Most of the people living in the apartment complex were college students, so Lucas and his roommate, Marc, wouldn't have to worry about the noise level too much. Lucas had been able to save up a lot of money by packing his things away in a small storage unit while he was gone and not pay rent. He said that he knew he'd want a house one day, so he split up his extra money between saving for a house and getting ahead on his retirement fund. Amanda learned a lot about retirement from talking to Lucas and was glad she was hoping to take advantage of a school district's matching IRA donations when she got hired.

Lucas was gone for Thanksgiving and went to spend Christmas with his father and his new wife, who had two teenage boys. He then spent three months in Oklahoma while Amanda was student teaching, but came back just before she started going on job interviews. She was hoping to teach at her alma mater, but she had to keep her options open. For student teaching, her assignment was to work with the high school English teacher at the school district that had a huge population of military children. Amanda was assigned to work with Mrs. Trunker at Spanaway Lake High School. Mrs. Trunker let Amanda truly teach the three afternoon classes twice a week with a project Amanda organized. She picked a different book with each class and assigned them to read a chapter a week. They had one discussion class and one writing class that tied to the book. Mrs. Trunker gave her solid feedback every day and helped her with some of the tougher students. A few kids with parents in the Army hadn't seen one of their parents for almost eight months as they were on a year-long deployment. One girl, Stephanie, was living with her neighbor since both of her parents were gone.

Amanda suggested starting an after-school tutoring session for a few of those students, and Mrs. Trunker arranged the details with the school and parents. Amanda started really looking forward to the tutoring days on Tuesdays and Thursdays.

Lucas loved hearing her stories about teaching and tutoring. They ended up talking on the phone almost every day while he was in Oklahoma. She was still working at the coffee shop on the weekends and some evenings to help her get through the summer. She was planning to move into an apartment before the school year started but wanted to make sure she had a teaching contract in place first. She wanted to live closer to downtown Tacoma, near the water, but also didn't want to commute too far. In April, there were three high school teaching jobs in the area, and Amanda applied for all three. There was one in Spanaway, one in Tacoma, and one in Lakewood. She wanted the one in Lakewood because it was a seventh and eighth grade teacher, and the pay was the best of the three jobs. It was also closer to the water and Tacoma than Spanaway. She also thought it would be a good distance from Lucas' apartment, which was near the fairgrounds in Puyallup.

Amanda finally heard back from the schools just two weeks before graduation. She was offered the job at Tacoma and Lakewood, but not at Spanaway. She accepted the job in Lakewood and was able to sign the contract the morning of graduation. Her parents held a party that evening, and while it would be pretty small with just her two aunts and uncles coming, a few friends, and a few of the kids from Mrs. Trunker's classes, Lucas had taken the day off, or "leave" as they said in the military, and would be with her all day. Juliana would be graduating the same day in Boston, and they planned their own celebration in two weeks – Juliana and Amanda were going to Paris for a week. Juliana's parents had given her the trip to Paris with a friend as a graduation gift, and Juliana had picked Amanda in a heartbeat. She had no trouble getting the time off work at Coffee First – Jodie was almost as excited as Amanda about her going. Amanda was glad she already had her passport from when her parents took her to Canada after eighth grade. She had a one more year until it needed to be renewed.

Her family gave her money as a graduation gift since they knew she was planning to move into an apartment and would need to furnish it. Her students had taken a blank book and passed it around for each kid to write her a letter. When they gave it to her, she quickly realized she would have to read it later as she started to tear up after reading the first two entries. She would treasure those letters for a long time and made sure they knew she really appreciated the gift. Mrs. Trunker gave her a teacher supply kit, full of items Amanda would need for her own classroom. Lucas gave her a hand-carved nameplate to put on her desk at school. It said "Ms. Schaffer," and he had carved a dragonfly after her name. She smiled when she saw that, knowing he had remembered her saying she could watch dragonflies all day when they had seen one at the park a few weeks ago.

Lucas said his goodbyes to her family right after they served cake. He had to be up early to leave on another trip. Amanda walked him to his car.

"Thank you for being here today – all day," she said.

"I'm so glad I could. It's a very important day. You should be so proud. I am," he said.

"I can't believe I won't see you for three weeks or more," she said. He wouldn't be back from his trip before she and Juliana left for Paris.

"You'll have so much fun, though," he said. "This time, you can bring me a present."

He gave her a long kiss, and she watched him drive away before heading back into the house. She planned to put a letter in the mail to him so he would have something when he got back. While she knew she'd have a great time with Juliana, she couldn't help but wish she was going to Europe with Lucas.

Amanda loved Paris. Juliana fulfilled her promise to not pay attention to any guys during the trip unless they could use it to their advantage, like getting escorted to the Mona Lisa right when the Louvre opened so they wouldn't have to wait in line, or the free gelato they got after dinner most nights. Amanda's favorite place was Versailles. She could imagine Marie Antoinette or Napoleon walking on the same marble steps where she was putting her feet. They spent the whole afternoon walking through the gardens before taking the train back to their hotel. On their last day, they went shopping for an outfit each just so when they got compliments on it, they could tell people they bought it in Paris. To end the day and the trip, they watched the sunset from the top of the Eiffel Tower.

Amanda didn't sleep well on the flight home. She had started mulling over the possibility of living somewhere outside of Washington State, something she had never really considered, even with seeing parts of the U.S., Mexico, and Canada. Europe was so different, and she finally understood the allure of living somewhere new where she didn't know every restaurant, tourist attraction, or historical marker. It had been fun to just explore Paris. Maybe that was the difference – she was able to enjoy and explore and not just learn about history and science like she did on her parents' summer trips.

She thought about Lucas a lot, too. She thought every night about what she would want to tell him about her day, but she was too tired to even write it down. While she had always been understanding about his lack of communication while on trips, she now truly understood how the days could get away from you while traveling and seeing new places. She would tell him that soon, but during the plane ride she jotted down notes to help her remember everything she wanted to tell him. He was picking Amanda and Juliana up from the airport and driving them each home. Their parents had dropped them off, but they weren't arriving home until 11:32 p.m. Lucas had offered and Amanda had accepted, not realizing until later that he had blocked the time off as official leave so he wouldn't get sent on a trip. She had tried to change his mind, saying one of their parents would be able to pick them up, but he said he really wanted to do it and he actually had to use some leave soon or it would be taken back.

She finally fell asleep during the last two hours of the flight. Juliana had been out the whole time. Once they got through customs, they made their way to the exit. Lucas was waiting right on the other side.

"Welcome home, girls," he said as he walked up to give them both hugs. Then, he grabbed just Amanda to give her a hug and quick kiss. When he let her go, he grabbed their suitcases. "I'll pull your luggage to the curb and then go bring the car around so you guys don't have to walk."

"Thank you," Juliana replied, sounding very awake.

Amanda tried to keep her eyes open for the ride home, but found herself waking up to the sound of the door closing after Juliana left the car. Lucas helped her take her suitcase to the house and then came back to take Amanda home.

"Sorry," she said sheepishly as he got in. "I didn't mean to fall asleep. I didn't sleep much on the flight."

"Don't worry about it. Your snore is actually quite cute."

"I don't snore!"

"Well, I'll show you the video I took if you go out to dinner with me tomorrow, and we can settle it then."

"I'm sure it was just noise from your car, but yes, I'll go out with you tomorrow. How about I call you when I wake up?"

"Sounds good," he said and then they stopped in her driveway. Lucas took her suitcase to the front porch and gave her a long goodnight kiss.

"I'm glad you're back. It was strange for me to be here and you to be gone."

"Yes, it was for me, too. But it was such a fun trip," Amanda yawned, "which I'll tell you about tomorrow. Must get sleep."

"Goodnight, my little traveler," he said.

Lucas almost had a normal schedule, if only in the fact that it was regular, after Amanda got back from Paris. He would be gone for about two weeks and home for a week, then it would repeat. He had started taking a few online classes while she was in Paris, which enabled him to sign in and do the work while he was on the road. He was studying finance. A college near a large military base in Nebraska offered the entire degree online, designed to be flexible for military personnel. It would all be paid for by the Air Force, too, which sounded great to Amanda.

Amanda split her time that summer between Coffee First, the tutoring center, and developing her plan for the upcoming school year. She saw Lucas when he was in town, but spent a lot of time with Juliana who would be going back to MIT for an 18-month intensive master's degree program that promised to get her a job with any big company out East. Her dream was to live in New York City or Chicago, and she was on track to do just that. Juliana helped Amanda with her apartment hunting in July. Amanda planned to move out the beginning of August so she could celebrate her 22nd birthday in her own place. Her birthday was August 7, and Lucas had just missed it last year because of the deployment. He had bought her "birthday plus one month flowers" on September 7, which she had thought was sweet.

Amanda's apartment was barely put together in time for the party. Juliana contacted any of their high school friends who were still in town, Lucas invited some of his work buddies, and Amanda asked a few friends from the teaching program who were planning to work in the local area. It was a luau-themed party with food, music, and karaoke. There were a few drinks available, and a lot of food. She had lucked out to find an apartment on the first floor, and her back door opened to a decent-sized concrete patio and a grassy area. It was only 50 feet away from the apartment complex's volleyball court, so that was an option for people as well. Since she only had a small couch, Amanda borrowed lawn chairs from her parents.

Amanda didn't get to chat with Lucas much during the party, but he had been around all day helping her get ready. She tried to make it around to talk to everyone at the party. She had requested no one bring any presents, but was collecting new socks for the local homeless shelter. There was a huge pile by the front door, and she wanted to thank people personally for bringing them. Lucas had brought a dozen packages, along with some flowers. Amanda had talked to about everyone inside at one point, so she stepped outside to see who was hanging out there. A volleyball game was going on, and several people were standing near the court watching. Juliana and two friends from high school were sitting in their chairs on the porch talking about their job situations.

Amanda started toward the volleyball court and saw Lucas, his roommate, and two other guys standing by the court. They were all smoking, which surprised Amanda. She had never seen Lucas smoke before.

"I can't wait to get back to Italy," one guy said.

"That was the best stop ever. There and Thailand, I've heard, are the only two places to get the good massages," Lucas' roommate replied.

"Plus the clubs are all topless in Europe," another guy said.

"Yeah, it's a great life," Lucas chimed in.

Amanda turned around and went back into her apartment. Did she really just hear her boyfriend talk about topless clubs and massages? And smoking? She thought to herself that she really shouldn't be surprised – he was in the military after all. She got herself a glass of wine and joined the people singing karaoke inside. She would try to put it out of her mind for tonight since it was her birthday, but she'd have to talk to him about it soon. When the party ended, she said a quick goodbye to Lucas as he walked out with his buddies. They were going to go to a place to shoot pool. He had asked her to come along, but she said she was tired. Juliana was the last one left and decided to crash there to help Amanda clean up in the morning. Amanda just wanted to put the food away before crawling into bed. She started to talk to Juliana about what she heard while she was putting the food away, but when there was a pause for Juliana to respond, it was quiet. Amanda peaked around the door to the living room from the kitchen and saw Juliana fast asleep on the couch. It would all have to wait until tomorrow. Despite how much it was bothering her, Amanda fell asleep almost as soon as she lay down.

"Why don't you call him now before I have to leave to get ready for work?" Juliana asked when they were both finally awake the next morning.

"It's only 8:30. He's probably still asleep."

"Well, then he won't be able to think up any lies." Juliana grabbed Amanda's phone and started looking up Lucas' number. When she found it, she handed it to Amanda. "Here, just hit call."

Amanda stared at the phone for a minute and then took it from Juliana. She hit call and listened to it ring and ring. It went to voicemail.

"Give me a call when you get this. There's something I want to talk to you about. Bye."

Amanda knew her voice sounded curt, and Lucas would know something wasn't right.

Juliana looked disappointed that Lucas hadn't picked up, but instead of dwelling on it, they spent the next half hour cleaning up the apartment from the party. It wasn't that bad, but there was some litter scattered in the grass out back. All Amanda had left was the bathroom and vacuuming when Juliana left for work. They had plans in a few days to have dinner at Phyllos before Juliana left again. They both knew it was most likely the last time they would live near each other for a very long time, but they had talked about taking a big trip together every few years just to stay close.

Amanda had the weekend off for her birthday – she decided to go shopping, get lunch from her favorite deli, and then come home and read on her back porch. Her parents were taking her out to dinner that night, and her Aunt Vicky was coming from Spokane. Lucas didn't call until right as she was leaving for dinner, so she let it go to voicemail. She didn't have time for a long discussion and just wanted to enjoy the evening. She listened to his message on her way to her parents' house.

"Amanda, hey, I'm sorry I didn't call back earlier. I left my phone in Marc's car and didn't realize it until just a little bit ago. We didn't get home until 4 a.m., but I won $100 playing pool. You sound upset, so please call me back soon. I hope I didn't do anything stupid."

Amanda didn't check her phone again until she got back in her car at her parents' house after dinner. Her aunt had announced she was pregnant and they would be moving closer as her husband, Uncle Eddie, was being transferred to Seattle. They were going to look at houses south of the city so they would be closer to her parents. Vicky and her mom were sisters, and they spent most of the dinner talking about the baby. Her aunt had given her a really nice personal planner that was designed for teachers. It was something that would come in very handy soon.

She had three missed calls from Lucas but no more voicemails. She decided to wait until she got home to decide whether to call him back or not. She noticed someone sitting on the step leading up to the second floor by her apartment when she pulled into the parking lot. She wasn't sure, but the height looked like it could be Lucas. She put two keys through her fingers in one hand and made a fist while holding her cell phone in the other – just in case she needed to protect herself. The figure stood when she was just a few feet away from her car and she relaxed – it was Lucas.

"Hi, Amanda," he said in a quiet voice. "I was hoping you'd be back here before too long. I got alerted this afternoon and have a lot of laundry to do before leaving Monday."

"Where to this time? Italy? Thailand?" she couldn't help but ask right away. His eyes quickly showed recognition to knowing what conversation she was referring to.

"Amanda, I swear I don't do those things. The guys were just talking, and I don't like to make a point of being different all the time."

"Is that why you were smoking, too?" Amanda unlocked her door so they could continue their conversation inside.

"I do smoke occasionally, but only about a dozen times a year when I'm hanging out with the guys and we're at a bar or shooting pool. That's something I can easily quit if it bothers you."

"I just didn't know that about you," she said.

"Here, let me do something for you." He pulled out his phone and sent a text to someone. They waited in silence for a minute until a "ping" sounded for a reply coming through. He handed her his phone:

> Lucas: Need a favor. Can you explain my nickname and why I have it so I can show it to Amanda.

> Marc: Nerd. You always go back and read when we go out to the clubs on trips.

"Really?" Amanda asked. "Nerd?"

"You can ask him in person when you see him next, but, yes, really. That'll be my second confession tonight. I read a lot."

He reached for her hand, and she let him hold it. She was mostly relieved but still a little upset in the revelation that there was still a lot to learn about Lucas and it was hard to get a real picture when he was gone a lot. He could easily hide things from her if he wanted. She didn't like thinking about that. She finally looked up at him and saw nothing but care and concern in his eyes. The bad feelings went away when she saw that, and she smiled. He had never really given her any good reason not to trust him, but she would be a little more watchful and cautious now. She needed to get to know him better, and it felt like their relationship moved in slow motion with him being gone so often. He pulled her in, and she let him just hold her for a while. When he let her go, he grabbed her hand and looked at her.

"Amanda, I see what some of these guys do on the road. I'm not naive, and I know you're not either. It can't be easy to be in a relationship with someone who is gone a lot and you don't see that often. It's not easy for me not being able to see what you do day in and day out, either. But I would never do something to intentionally hurt you. Please trust me."

"I do, Lucas. I just feel we really need to get to know each other much better," she said.

"I have an idea that might help that."

They started writing each other a letter before each trip for the other to read when Lucas was gone. Lucas had found a list of 100 questions in a magazine to ask the person you're dating, and they answered a few in each letter. Amanda read her first letter from Lucas each night and would jot down questions she had on the envelope. When she showed it to him when he got back, he admitted to reading her letter every night, too. He loved the idea of writing questions on the envelope. He had a few for her. They stayed up really late the first night he was back asking each other the questions. Amanda could feel their relationship moving at a faster pace over the next few months with the help of the letters. The more she got to know Lucas – his likes, dislikes, childhood memories, and plans for the future – the more she liked him as a person and the harder she wished that he wasn't in the military.

CHAPTER ELEVEN

Amanda loved teaching even more than she thought she would. The week before school started was full of meetings, training, and getting her classroom decorated and organized. One other person from her college was also teaching pre-calculus and calculus at the same school. Trent Mitchell wasn't very social, but as the only two new teachers that year, they sat together during the meetings and training sessions.

On the first day of school, a Wednesday, she had a fun icebreaker game for each class, which gave her a good overview of the students' personalities and social statuses. She took lots of notes on her "Who has ...?" paper so she could make good seating arrangements that night. Each student also filled in a questionnaire for her that would fill in the blanks for her on what activities and sports they participated in, if they had siblings or parents in the district, and some of their likes and dislikes. She had just enough time to pass out and quickly go over the syllabus for each class, too. She had three seventh grade and three eighth grade classes and a homeroom that was the last period and had a combination of both grades. Lucas had a night flight that night, so they planned to go out on Friday to dinner and a movie to celebrate. She found flowers waiting at her door when she got home that night with a note from Lucas.

Amanda,
I'm glad to be able to watch you fulfill your dreams. You are a great teacher and will influence many lives. Proud of you!
Love,
Lucas

Amanda put the flowers in the middle of her kitchen table, took the card, and sat down on the couch to read it over a few more times. It was the first time he had used the word "love," and she couldn't chalk it up to the florist accidentally writing it because the card was in his own all-caps print handwriting. They had been dating for almost a year and a half now and were easily calling each other boyfriend and girlfriend. Did she love him? She knew she didn't want him to leave and missed him when he was on trips. Was that love? She wanted to call Juliana, but she knew this was something she had to figure out on her own. She propped the card in the kitchen as she made dinner and put it on the table while she ate. Finally, as she put it on her nightstand while getting ready for bed and read it for about the thousandth time, she said out loud, "Lucas, I love you, too." She smiled. That was easy, and while it felt true and right, she knew she'd have no trouble saying it to his face even though she'd never really told a guy that before.

She decided to tell him that Friday. As they were saying goodbye at her apartment door, he whispered as he pulled away from a kiss, "Good night, Amanda. I love you."

She whispered it back quickly, before she could even think about it, and was rewarded with a long kiss. He looked back at her and smiled at least three times as he walked to his car that night. Amanda knew she'd have to call Juliana the next day and tell her. Things with Lucas had finally moved over to the serious relationship category, and now Amanda was truly involved, with all her heart, with a military man. Despite all her best intentions and knowing that the military life was hard, here she was. Oh, why did this good man, this man she loved, have to be in the military?

Lucas flew to Florida to spend Thanksgiving with his mom, and Amanda went with her parents to spend it with her Aunt Vicky and Uncle Eddie. The weather was nice, so they all spent Black Friday in downtown Seattle and took a boat tour. Vicky spotted two seals as they were turning back into the harbor and declared it was a sign – she should decorate the nursery with seals. Eddie was sweet and told her they could do it anyway she wanted, they just had to finish by March with the baby due in April.

The next weekend, Lucas took her to the restaurant in Seattle they had originally planned to go to on their second date. It was a Saturday, and while he had made reservations, they left three hours ahead of time just to make sure traffic wouldn't deter them. They could walk along the water if they had time to kill, which they did. Lucas had bought a few new CDs, and they spent most of the drive checking out the newest country music releases.

"I have some news I need to tell you," Lucas said shortly after they began strolling along the water. She looked up at him, but they continued walking.

"We had a commander's call this week and ... I'm really beginning to hate those things," he paused for almost a minute and she just walked and waited for the news. "We have another deployment coming up in April for six months."

They both stopped and just looked at each other for a few minutes. She couldn't imagine him being gone for that long again – so soon.

"I thought you said when you came back that they were going to try to keep those about three years apart? You just came back a little over a year ago."

"That's what they had told us," he said as they resumed walking. He grabbed her hand and squeezed it tight. "A few months ago, the higher ups decided to change how the flow of squadron deployments went since a few new squadrons are being added. The new ones got sent to the end of the list, and ours got moved to the top. They said we had the people and the training and that they promised it would be on a three-year cycle after that."

"That really doesn't seem fair," she said.

"It isn't," he said. "I also have to let you know one other thing. When I get back, it will only be a few months until I will get orders to move."

Amanda felt a tear escape the corner of her eye. Her first instinct was to run back to the car, but then she looked at him and they fell into an embrace.

Several more tears escaped before she was ready to let him go.

He reached up and wiped the tears from her cheeks. She took her glasses off and cleaned them on her shirt. As she put them back on, he put a hand on her shoulder.

"We'll figure this all out, Amanda. It's not great news, but we can figure a way to get through it. That is, if you want to."

At first she was surprised by what he said. She had forgotten she had a choice. She didn't have to stay in a relationship with a man who wouldn't be there for long. But, she knew in her heart she wanted to try. She couldn't let this man go just because the military required him to leave.

"I do, Lucas. Somehow we'll figure this all out." He kissed her and held her hand as they walked slowly back to the restaurant in silence to make their dinner reservation. They both tried at first to keep the conversation light, but they ended up talking about how to stay in touch during the deployment. They would give each other a small present to open on their birthdays. Lucas' was in May. Amanda said she would find a different list of questions they could go through when he had the chance to email. With that all settled, they moved on to talking about their week. Neither of them mentioned the possibility of Lucas moving when he got back. A deployment separation was enough to face that night.

"So, what it sounds like is that you have at least an entire year before he'd be moving anywhere else? That's actually a lot of time," Juliana said on the phone that night. Amanda called her as soon as she was back in the apartment, even though she knew it would be late. Juliana wouldn't mind.

"It sounds like it, but he'll also be gone for half of that."

"I was just reading an article last week about how long-distance relationships tend to last longer because the two people have to be good at communicating."

"So you don't think this would be grounds for thinking of possibly ending the relationship?"

"Amanda, I've seen the two of you together. You might as well realize that you are in love with a military man, despite saying you were never going to do such a thing."

Amanda sighed. "Why does he have to be in the military?"

"Maybe it's God's way of keeping the universe in check. It seems he likes it when people say 'Never' so he can make sure it does happen."

"True, true," Amanda laughed. "I do know there is no way I could move in the middle of a school year, though."

"You shouldn't have to. Even if he moves in the school year, you could stay and he could get a place set up. He wouldn't be there half of that time anyway, so it would be your turn to be somewhere you wanted, like when he's deployed."

"You're right. The military doesn't have to determine my life schedule – just the one of the man I'm dating."

"Remember, too, Amanda, while you guys are serious, you're not engaged yet, and you said he hasn't brought up marriage at all, even when he told you about possibly moving. Don't plan too far ahead, especially if he's not. You don't need to move across the country unless he's your husband."

"I guess I'm only really thinking about it now. I'd want some kind of decision like that before he moves, though. Long-distance dating with no end in sight is definitely not something I'm game for."

"Good. Watch out for yourself. Um, hey, can I tell you about Brian real quick?"

"Brian? Who's Brian? Tell me."

Juliana then told Amanda all about a guy she had been dating for a solid month now. He was also in the structural engineering intensive master's program, and he was from Colorado. Juliana had never dated a guy more than a few weeks at any time, so this was a big deal. Amanda noted she sounded more excited about Brian than most guys, too. She loved that he was smart and honestly sought out her opinions and thoughts on things, expecting her to be as smart or smarter than he was. She was always quick to dump any guy who talked down to her or thought she had gotten into a tough program because of her looks. Amanda smiled as she thought about Juliana actually having a possible long-term boyfriend as she hung up the phone. It had also been a nice distraction from thinking about Lucas.

Over the next few months, Amanda and Lucas talked about the deployment, but never about the move except for one time, while having dinner at his apartment with Marc and his newest date. He tended to only date someone once or twice before moving on to someone else. Amanda had asked if there were only certain locations they could move to with their job in the military or if they could go anywhere.

"They like to send us younger guys to Altus or Hawaii since not as many families want to go there," Marc said.

"They like to go to Charleston," Lucas said. "I did hear they might be sending some up to Alaska soon, though."

"Alaska?" Marc's date asked. "I'd never live up there – I don't like snow!"

"It's beautiful up there," Amanda said. "Where's Altus?"

"It's in Oklahoma. There's also New Jersey and that base in Northern California," Lucas said. "Only the really special dudes get picked for the Dover assignment."

"I heard they don't have to do the trips all the time, either," Marc said.

"Wouldn't that be nice? Or maybe the war could end sometime soon and these planes could get a break," Lucas replied. He and Marc spent most of the rest of dinner talking about how it wasn't right how much they were gone and the wear and tear to the airplanes. Eventually, they were all sharing work stories, but Amanda had the information she needed about what the future could possibly hold. None of the locations were awful, except for maybe Oklahoma. Northern California would be really close, and even Alaska was a frequent destination for people leaving SeaTac. The East Coast seemed very far away, but Amanda remembered the adventure of Paris and knew she could enjoy a new location, if life were to take her that way. Although she was really glad he didn't say anywhere overseas. She wasn't quite that adventurous and wanted to be able to go see her family easily if she wanted. She also really didn't want to experience a foreign country by herself if he would still be gone a lot while they were there.

The next few months seemed to pass quickly between work, spending time with Lucas, and trying to finish the project she was working on for him to take on his deployment. He told her that the Internet connection was much better over there now, so he would be able to contact her on a more regular basis. She knew there would be times when he was busy or flying, though, so she wanted to create something that would keep them connected. She bought two, 180-page journals, one black and one white. The white one was for her to keep track of things that happened each day that she wanted to share with him. The black one was for Lucas. She had gone through and put dates on the top of each page and she was also going through his to put a small encouraging note, quote, or picture on each page, hoping they would make each day a little brighter for him. They would be able to exchange notebooks when he got back and spend some time catching up on each other's lives without forgetting things.

Lucas had taken her to a pre-deployment meeting for families, spouses, and loved ones. A lot of the topics didn't apply to them because they weren't married, but Amanda learned a lot more about what they would actually be doing during the deployment, why they had to take a turn again so soon, and how to send Lucas care packages. They were at a table that seemed like it was just for the guys who had serious girlfriends – just four couples. The three other women and Amanda shared contact information and planned a small get together for two weeks after the guys left. They all liked romantic comedies and decided they would have a movie club once a month to watch the movies the guys wouldn't want to see anyway. It sounded like fun.

Amanda also ran into Terri, who was pregnant, during a break while getting something to drink.

"Hi, there. It was Amy, wasn't it?"

"Amanda, actually," she said with a smile and moved her hair from her name tag.

"I'm glad you're here. Have you signed up on the spouses list?"

"Well, I'm not a spouse yet. Just a girlfriend," Amanda replied.

"Oh, sorry. But that doesn't really matter. During a deployment, we always welcome the girlfriends to our events since you're going through a lot of the same things we are and you sometimes have less support. Let me get the sign-up sheet. Where are you sitting?"

"I'm in the back with the rest of the girlfriends," Amanda said and pointed to her table. Lucas saw her and waved.

"Oh, good, I can get all of you. Bethie will like that. She's the commander's wife," Terri said and then walked off to get the sign-up list. Amanda went back to her table. Terri came soon after and got all four women to write down their contact information, making sure to note that they were girlfriends and not spouses. She told them there would be monthly social events, a book club, a few Seattle shopping trips, and times to get together and put care packages together. She would make sure they were added to the email list and sent a calendar. Most of the activities would be on base, so they would have to call one of the key spouses at least a day ahead of time to get their names put on the visitor list for the gate guard. It sounded slightly complicated to Amanda, but she was interested in helping with the care packages, so she was determined to figure it out.

When they left the meeting, Amanda had a list of questions for Lucas, mostly acronyms that she didn't understand. She felt like she was entering a new world that had its own secret language.

They said goodbye after having dinner at Phyllos. He had a 4 a.m. show time, and told her it would be easier to do it that way. When she pulled out the journal to give him, he laughed.

"Okay, clue me in – how is a journal funny?"

"It's not funny, but getting a journal was one of the last things I had to run out and get tonight to pack," he said.

"Really? You journal?"

"I do. I started doing it in high school. I bought a notebook for the last deployment to keep that separate from my usual journals, so this is perfect."

"I had no idea you did that. I don't think a lot of guys do."

"It was actually a challenge from an English teacher in 10th grade. He asked us to journal at least three times a week to get some writing inspiration. If we showed him our journal entries on Fridays, he would give us extra credit. I always did any extra credit that was offered. After that year, I was just in the habit of doing it, and I liked being able to go back and see how I've changed over the years."

"Well, I don't really journal, but I bought myself one to use during this deployment. I thought we could share our journals when you got back in case there's anything we forgot to tell each other."

"Amanda, I love it! Thank you. I'll miss you a lot, but it will help to 'talk' to you every day in the journal."

"I'm going to miss you, too."

Amanda kept herself busy that summer by teaching some summer school classes in Tacoma and tutoring three high school girls who were referred to her from her father. She didn't miss the early mornings at the coffee shop, but she did try to make it there at least every other week to see Jodie and catch up with her. During the school year, she had been able to go early a few times and bring drinks in for the other English teachers, too. She was slowly getting to know them, but it was hard to feel like she belonged some days when they had worked together for 12 years and she had only been there for one. Bringing in their favorite coffee drinks had gone a long way toward getting them talking to her more, though.

Lucas was able to video chat with Amanda four times while he was gone for about 15 minutes. They had scheduled time slots each month, and he had been on trips for two of them. He was training for a full marathon this time and lifting more weights. She could see the difference in the video chats. He said he was mainly doing it to stay busy. Between the trips, staying caught up on class work, and working out, he didn't have much time to just sit and complain, which wasn't anything he wanted to do anyway. They would both have to break their new "staying busy" habits when he got back in October. Amanda planned to not do any tutoring in the fall, and Lucas had his marathon run on Halloween, so he would be done with that training by then.

"What costume should I wear for the run?" he asked her in their last video chat in September.

"What about C3PO since you're so tall? Or a tree?" she tried to keep a straight face, but burst out laughing thinking of him running dressed as a tree.

"Well, those would be fun," he said, smiling, "but I do have to be able to run in the costume. What about Spiderman? Or a guy from the Blue Man Group?"

"There's bound to be a lot of those since that fits into a typical running getup. Hmmm, what about running in a kilt? My dad has one of those leprechaun hats that has a red beard attached to it. You could be the tallest Irishman around."

"That would be fun. Maybe I'll do that. Can you see if you dad would let me borrow the hat? I actually think Marc might have a kilt since his high school mascot was the Scots. It was their dress uniform for away football games."

"No way! I've never heard of that. That's hilarious!" They both had a good laugh picturing Marc in a kilt and then their time was almost up.

"Amanda, thanks for taking my call. It's been a tough two days. I found out when I got back yesterday that one of the guys at the fitness center committed suicide. They're saying his wife sent him a letter saying she was going to ask for a divorce when he got home and move to Texas with their two kids. It's just so sad."

"Oh, Lucas, that is so very sad. He must have felt hopeless."

"It gets hard for all of us being gone for so long, but the chaplains are really good about being there if people need to talk. I'm definitely going to pay more attention to the guys I'm around, though."

Amanda saw a hand tap Lucas' shoulder – the signal that his time was officially up and it was someone else's turn to connect with a loved one.

"I gotta go, but I get to see you in 27 days – in person!"

"I can't wait," Amanda said and she blew him a kiss. He blew one back.

"Love you."

"Love you, too."

Lucas came back on a Friday, and Amanda was able to get the day off after the principal stepped in. She hadn't taken any days off since she started working the year before, but the English department chair didn't want her to have the day off because it was full of end-of-quarter tests and they didn't like to have substitutes on those days. She recommended no, but when the principal saw why Amanda was taking the day off, she approved it. She sent Amanda an email to let her know and told her she had a nephew who was on his third deployment and that it was important we showed support to the troops. Amanda immediately replied with a "thank you." The English chair came into her room shortly after that and told her she really had wanted to say yes, but she had to follow the recommendations. She said she was glad the principal had approved the request. Amanda was relieved to hear that – she didn't want to have any problems with any other teachers, although it would have been worth it to see Lucas when he got home.

By the time Lucas got back, Amanda felt like a pro going onto the base. She went once or twice a month during the deployment to a spouse social or a care package packing party. She no longer felt like the gate guards were scrutinizing her every move as she drove up. She had even survived a car inspection in May. She had no idea what they would be looking for, but she had hoped they wouldn't find it. It only took them five minutes to look her car over as she never kept much in it and then they wished her a good day.

When she walked into Base Ops, she saw several familiar faces but walked over to Terri first and looked at her new baby. They had been able to send her husband back home for the birth, and he helped run things at the office for the end of the deployment. They were both there, along with their other son.

"He is just so adorable," Amanda said. "I know I say that every time I see you, but he just seems like the sweetest baby."

"Thanks! I think it's all because his father is home to have a calming effect on us all," she replied. "I'm so excited to see all the guys coming back home. I truly hope it's another three years before they have to go again."

"Isn't that what they've been promised?" Amanda asked.

"Yes, but the military doesn't always keep its promises. We get our orders next month to move in January. If we get Alaska, Will won't have to deploy for a couple years. If we get Altus, he'll be home all the time. If we get Charleston, several of those squadrons are up for deployments next year."

"Oh, I hadn't thought about that," Amanda said. "So, deployments are based on the squadron, not on the person? That makes sense, of course, I just hadn't thought about it that way. Lucas said he would get orders soon, too, after the deployment."

"I didn't mean to upset you. It's good for you to know how it works, though. Women should think hard before they sign up to be a military wife. My father was in the military, so I knew what I was getting into, but so many of these marriages end early because the wife wasn't prepared for the TDYs, trips, and deployments."

The commander started speaking then, and Amanda thought about what Terri had said. She wasn't concentrating on what the commander was saying until she heard the word "suicide."

"There were two suicides on the base our squadron was stationed at for the deployment. One just happened five days ago, so you may not have been told about that from your loved one yet. I wanted to let you know so you can give your loved one extra support if they seem to be affected. The first one worked at the fitness center, and many in the unit came in contact with him often. The other was a maintenance worker who fixed issues with the planes we flew. While there wasn't as much interaction with him, it was someone closely tied to our mission.

"Capt. Lauder will hand out a flyer here in a minute that lists all the support services offered to military members coming back from a deployment. The chaplains are always available. Father Brown is here with us today. Family Services and the hospital offer counseling. Please call me anytime if there are ever any serious issues. My number is written on the back of the pamphlets."

He then started to discuss all the accomplishments of the squadron during the deployment. Amanda was handed a pamphlet, and she decided to put the commander's number in her phone – just in case. She glanced over the pamphlet and then tucked it into her purse. Like Terri said, she should know what she was getting into. Then the guys started coming through the double doors.

Lucas was about the 25th guy to come through the doors, not that Amanda had been counting, she said to herself. This time, she walked toward him, and he ran toward her. They embraced and then he dipped her down for a kiss like the iconic World War II reunion photo. He pulled her up, and the whole room clapped. She could feel her face turning red, but a huge smile was beaming across her face. They walked hand-in-hand to her car. They went to get a quick late lunch at a local burger joint just outside of the base gate, and while they both smiled a lot, there wasn't a lot of talking as they were both hungry and it was obvious Lucas was tired. She took him to a hotel where he planned to stay for just a few days before moving back into the same apartment complex, just a different apartment and roommate. Marc was heading to training in Oklahoma in two weeks, so Lucas was going to share the space with Greg. Amanda hadn't met Greg as he had just moved to the base a few months before the deployment. It was his second assignment, so he was older than Lucas by just a few years.

There was a squadron party the next night, and her family had Lucas over for Sunday brunch to welcome him home. Their first real date with time to themselves would be Sunday night – at Phyllos.

CHAPTER TWELVE

Phyllos was not a fancy dinner location, but Lucas asked her to dress up a little in case they went somewhere else downtown after dinner. He said he had a surprise in store, but that's all he would tell her. When he picked her up, he was actually in tan slacks, brown dress shoes, a long-sleeved blue button-up shirt, and a dark red tie.

"You've only dressed up like this for the two times we headed to the restaurant in Seattle," she noted as they walked to his car from her apartment. "We must be going somewhere really nice after dinner." She had guessed they might go see the play that was running in Tacoma, the off-Broadway show of "The Phantom of the Opera." They hadn't been to a play together yet, but she and Juliana tried to go to one every year.

"You'll see," he said with a wink and a grin.

Lucas talked about his trip home, and Amanda told him about work that week. She couldn't believe she had a student this year who kept slipping text talk into his essays. Lucas was a little more quiet than usual from what she remembered, but she knew he was probably still tired and jet-lagged.

When they got to Phyllos, Lucas parked right in front of the entrance. Amanda thought it was odd there were only a few cars in the parking lot. It was usually fairly packed, especially on the weekend. After Lucas opened her door and helped her out of the car, she saw the owner, Nicholas, open the door to let them in. Amanda thought that was odd, too, but Lucas led them to the door.

"Welcome! Welcome! What a beautiful night!"

As they walked in, Amanda realized they were the only two customers. The tables were rearranged so there was a small one in the middle of the restaurant decorated with candles and a lot of room around it. The lights were dimmed and the music playing was George Strait – one of the few music artists both Lucas and Amanda could agree was good. Amanda turned and looked at Lucas.

"What's all this?" she asked.

"Amanda, for sticking with me through two deployments now, you deserve a special night. I talked Nicholas into letting us have the restaurant to ourselves tonight. We're having a five-course Greek feast with all your favorites." He took both her hands in his. "Care to dance first?"

They danced for two songs and then sat down to dinner. Each course brought more of her favorites, and their conversation eased back to what was normal for them as they shared more stories of their lives from the past six months. Lucas had loved the journal and said some days it was the only thing that made him smile. They talked about the suicides for a bit and to Amanda, it seemed like Lucas was handling such sad events very well. When it was time for dessert, Lucas went back to the kitchen to ask for it as they hadn't seen Nicholas or his daughter, Nikki, for a while. He came back with tiramisu, but instead of placing it on the table, he held it out in his palm and got down on one knee beside her chair. Amanda saw a flash of light on top of the tiramisu and realized there was a ring on top. Amanda was shocked. She barely had time to turn and face him before he started talking.

"Amanda, I've been planning this since the day I stepped on that plane for the deployment. My heart didn't want to go, and I realized I felt home wherever you are. If you're willing to follow me around for a few years, we will settle down wherever you want when I leave the Air Force. Amanda, will you make my world complete and marry me?"

For a few seconds after he stopped talking, Amanda could only hear her heart beating. She felt scared, nervous, overjoyed and, yet, oddly sure of her answer.

"Yes," was all she could say and he took the ring off the tiramisu and put it on her finger. He pulled her up and kissed her before starting another dance to "I Cross My Heart." At the end of the song, Lucas turned her to face the kitchen area and there were her parents and Juliana, who had a camera with her. She smiled at Lucas and then ran over to hug each of them. She was so glad he thought to include them in this special moment.

"I got all the pictures," Juliana said. "The look on your face was priceless!"

Amanda fake punched Juliana's arm but laughed along with her. Enough tiramisu was brought out for all of them, along with some champagne. Amanda looked down at her engagement ring and chased away the thoughts in her head that made her wonder whether she really knew what she was getting into. She would enjoy this night and think about that tomorrow.

Amanda and Lucas quickly decided on a summer wedding so Amanda wouldn't have to miss teaching and they could go for a long two-week honeymoon to Hawaii. It was one of the few states Amanda hadn't been to in all her summer travels with her parents. Lucas was in charge of planning it as he had been there a handful of times and could get some military discounts for places to stay. Amanda asked Juliana to be her maid of honor, and Lucas was trying to pin down either a cousin of his who still lived in South Carolina or Marc to be his best man.

Most of the wedding details were left to Amanda as Lucas was gone on trips frequently. Lucas visited both his parents during the week of Christmas to tell them the news of their engagement in person and ask them to come to the wedding. His dad quickly agreed, but his mom said she'd have to see what her plans were as it got closer. Juliana came back during her Christmas break before her last semester of her intensive to help Amanda plan more details and so they could go dress shopping together with Amanda's mom. They spent a full day out, going to three different dress shops, including one in Seattle, and having brunch together. Juliana did the driving as there was actually a light dusting of snow that day, and she was used to driving in snow. Amanda thought the snow made the world look pretty and perfect.

"A white day for finding a white dress," she said as they drove into Seattle. They had eaten brunch there before heading to Brides Boutique. Amanda tried on three dresses at each of the Tacoma stores but found five options in Seattle. None of them struck her as "the dress" until she walked toward the mirror in the last dress. It was a solid white satin with a full Cinderella skirt. The sleeves were three-quarters length and there was a white rose embroidery around the bottom of the sleeves and the neckline. It was simple and elegant and perfect.

"Oh, Amanda, that dress fits you like a glove, and I think it's the best one yet," her mom said. "What do you think, Juliana?"

Juliana just smiled at Amanda and nodded her head. Amanda smiled back at her.

"This is my wedding dress," she declared and then she spun around a few times and they all laughed. "Let's get a picture together – just don't let Lucas see it!"

They were able to take the dress home. Amanda's mom would keep it at her house. They were offered a free alteration, if needed, before the wedding, so Amanda's mom said she would note in her calendar to have Amanda try it on in May. Amanda's hope was that it would either still fit or just need to be taken in a little. She had signed up for Zumba and spin classes at the local YMCA where the school district had an employee discount program. A few other teachers from the school went there, too, so she was making some other work friends that way. She knew a lot of her honeymoon would be spent in a swimsuit, so although she was on the skinny side, she wanted to make sure she looked fit when she got to Hawaii.

Lucas was gone to Europe for Valentine's Day, and when he picked her up to take her out on a make-up date, he wasn't in a good mood. She had learned over the months to let him talk about what was bothering him in his own time. When she started asking a lot of questions about his mood, he tended to close up even more, and it took so much longer for her to figure out what was bothering him. A few months ago when his roommate got sent to a military school and he had to find someone else to move in or pay the whole rent himself, she kept asking him questions and coming up with solutions. He snapped at her saying he couldn't even get a thought straight in his own head. He apologized right away and then explained how he liked to spend time thinking through problems on his own before talking to someone about it. He promised to get better about including her, though.

He asked her a few questions about her week while they drove to The Keg, but they mostly just listened to music. When they pulled into the parking lot, Lucas finally told her what was going on.

"I got my orders today," he said. "They are sending me to Charleston, but I have to go to school in Oklahoma en route to my new duty station."

"Moving to Charleston doesn't seem bad. You still have a few family members there, right?"

"Charleston will be fun, especially with you there with me. But, Amanda, the school in Altus starts in June, and I start work in Charleston the middle of August."

"What day does the class start?"

Lucas looked away from her and out the front windshield of the car. Both hands gripped the steering wheel.

"June 3."

Amanda's heart sank. That was only two days after they were planning on getting married – just about 50 yards from where they were parked. There was a gazebo on the water in a small park next to the restaurant. They planned to have the reception at The Keg since it was where they'd had their first date.

"Is there any way at all to change it? Did you tell them you were getting married?"

Lucas turned to her, and she could see he was as upset as she was about it. He reached out and grabbed her hand.

"I've been trying for two weeks to get it changed, and they even reached out to the other bases to see if anyone else could take the school slot so I could go to the next one, but no one can. They're either deployed, in the process of moving, or one guy's wife is due with their first child at that time."

"What are we going to do? You can't marry me and leave two days later. Do I come with you? Where would we live?"

"There are several options, but we are limited because for some of them, you aren't covered until we're actually married. Let's go inside, get a drink and order some food, and discuss them all. We will figure this out together," he said and then he gently put his hand under her chin and gave her a reassuring kiss. The thought went through her head again, "Why, God, did he have to be in the military?"

After discussing all their options, they decided to keep the wedding date the same. They would splurge and spend the night at the fanciest hotel in Seattle and then start the drive to Oklahoma together the next day. Lucas' things would be packed up for the move before the wedding, and Amanda would keep her apartment until early August. She would fly back to Washington two weeks before her lease was up to get things packed up and loaded on a truck. Lucas would drive to Charleston as soon as his class ended and then fly back to Seattle, hopefully by August 1. Then they would drive to Charleston together, stopping for some sightseeing along the way. They should then have some time to look for a place to live before Lucas started working. As soon as he got settled on the job and could take some leave, they would take the trip to Hawaii. By the end of the night, Amanda was almost excited for the adventure of it all and realized it was because she'd be doing it all with Lucas.

He also showed her some printouts of research he'd done on how she could get her teaching license in South Carolina. It all looked very doable over the next few months so that she could apply for jobs in the summer, if she wanted to work. Lucas said he wanted her to know that he would support her whether she was working or not. She couldn't imagine not teaching, though. Especially since it gave her something to do when he was on trips.

Amanda called Juliana that night and told her all the details. Juliana seemed relieved that Amanda and Lucas were able to figure out a plan.

"That does sound like quite an adventure for you," Juliana said. "Honestly, I don't know if I could have helped you figure it out much. I'm using up all my brain power on the papers and projects I have due in the next two months before I graduate."

"Have you been able to see Brian much?"

"Yes, he's the bright spot in all this! We are working together on two of the projects and have a study session for other classes a few nights a week. And, yes, we actually do study most of the time."

Amanda laughed at that, and they soon wrapped up the conversation. Amanda could tell Juliana's mind was elsewhere. She would tell her parents about the changes to the plan when she had dinner with them on Sunday.

"You're not even going on a honeymoon?" her mom asked.

"Well, we will eventually, but he has to be in Oklahoma two days after the wedding."

"Mr. Browan's brother owns The Renaissance in Seattle. I bet we can get you a discount rate there," her dad said. He seemed to be taking the announcement very well.

"You don't seem upset by this much, Charles," her mother said.

"You've seen how serious they've been getting, and he is in the military. I knew they'd have to move one of these days, and the two Reservists at our school have told numerous stories about how quickly some of these decisions are made," he replied.

"I can't believe you're going to move all the way across the country! Although, I guess that's where we'll be heading next summer for our vacation," her mom said. "Hilton Head was one of my favorite places when we'd head out to the East coast."

"I do have one big question for you, Dad," Amanda said as she turned to face him. "If for some reason Lucas can't fly back in time for me to move out of my apartment and start driving, will you go with me? I somehow have to get both the U-Haul and the car to South Carolina in August. Lucas should fly back to help me, but if his class runs longer, he might not. They have to do some flights as part of the class, and sometimes weather or maintenance cancels those and they have to add another day."

"Sure thing," her mom actually replied. "School doesn't start here until August 31 next year. Why don't you plan on me and your dad driving the U-Haul and either you or both you and Lucas drive the car? We're used to driving an RV, so the U-Haul would be no problem. Right, Charles?"

"That sounds like a good idea to me. We hadn't decided where to go this summer yet. We can do Hilton Head after we drop her off and then rent an RV to take home."

Her parents started talking about where they would want to stop on the way back, and Amanda smiled and hoped one day she and Lucas would be discussing memories of their travels across the country. She was so glad her parents agreed to help her move. It made it all seem less scary.

Amanda actually saw less of Lucas in the three months before their wedding than any other time when he'd been home. He had to arrange his move, get completely current in the plane, take his physical fitness test, go to doctor appointments, and do a lot of out-processing briefings, which would clear him from different offices as he left the base. He told her he'd have to repeat the process when they got to Charleston, but it would be called in-processing. She'd be able to go along to most of those. She kept herself busy with the last-minute wedding details. Juliana wouldn't fly in until the day before the wedding for the rehearsal dinner. She was in the process of moving herself. Both Juliana and Brian had gotten jobs at a firm in Chicago, and she would start loading up her own U-Haul the day after she flew back from the wedding. There seemed to be a million and one things that needed to be confirmed, and about every other item had something change or go wrong with it. Amanda's mom helped her as much as she could, but school was still in session, so they were both limited in the time they could spend talking to the vendors. Just when Amanda was ready to throw in the towel and elope or just not get married, Lucas suggested they take a day off and spend it in Seattle. They had done that about a year before and had both enjoyed it. It sounded wonderful to Amanda.

They wandered around the Experience Music Project and then had lunch at the top of the Space Needle. It was windy that day, so the Space Needle actually swayed a bit, which made them both a bit uneasy. They took pictures of each other at the top with the Victorian houses and Puget Sound in the background. In the afternoon, they wandered around Pike Place with coffees in hand from the original Starbucks. Lucas bought her a big bouquet of fresh flowers, and they sat for a caricature portrait. The artist made Lucas even taller and skinner and made Amanda's glasses larger and hair longer, but it still looked enough like them that anyone who knew them would recognize who it was. He drew the Space Needle in the background for them.

"This will have to hang up in our new house in Charleston," Lucas said. "Washington will always feel like home to me because it's where I met you."

"I think home is going to feel like being wherever you are," Amanda replied and gave him a kiss. "But, of course, I will always love Washington."

Amanda felt more ready to deal with the last two weeks of wedding hassle after that day with

Lucas. She felt more at peace, too, and knew marrying him was the right choice, even if she had to put up with the challenges of marrying a man in the military. Lucas made sure they had two more dinner dates on the calendar before the wedding, and they went to Phyllos both times. The rehearsal dinner was going to be there, too. They both loved the idea of celebrating there and supporting Nicholas since he'd done so much to help Lucas with the engagement. Amanda was glad it was a small wedding party so that they could all fit in the restaurant. Lucas ended up having his cousin as his best man, and Juliana met him at the rehearsal. Kevin was an auto mechanic in Georgia but had not moved there until high school. Kevin and Lucas were the same age and had spent most of their time in the summers together since they lived only three blocks apart. Those three blocks of separation put them in different schools, though, and they played against each other in sports.

It seemed that before she knew it, Amanda was getting ready at her mother's house for the wedding. A limo took her, her parents, and Juliana to the wedding site. Amanda stayed in the limo until it was time for her to walk down the red runner that ran from the sidewalk to the gazebo. She was able to watch Aunt Vicky and Uncle Eddie's baby, Alice, be the flower girl through the limo window. Vicky had to hold her as she threw the rose petals on the ground. As her father walked Amanda down the aisle, she noted that the sun was shining and there was not a cloud in the sky. What a perfect and rare day to get married in Washington! She looked at Lucas and saw his eyes were wide, and a huge smile was on his face. She smiled big in return and wished she could freeze the moment for a while and just enjoy the sunshine and the look on Lucas' face while she wore the perfect white dress. She kept moving forward, though, and her father handed her hand gently over to Lucas. Amanda barely paid attention to what the minister was saying and neither did Lucas. They were just staring and smiling. They wrote their own vows, but wanted to keep it simple.

"I, Amanda Lynn Schaffer, promise to spend my whole life loving you, Lucas Timothy Weston. My whole heart will be forever and completely yours as long I live."

"I, Lucas Timothy Weston, promise to give my all to love you with a love you deserve, Amanda Lynn Schaffer. My heart will only love you until the day I die."

Their rings matched and were actually three rings melded and woven together. Lucas had gotten them each a ring from Washington to represent where Amanda was from, from South Carolina to represent where Lucas was from, and from Turkey where Lucas said he was when he knew he was in love with her. He had collected the rings before he told her about the idea he had. He was nervous about what she would think, but she absolutely loved the idea of the rings being unique and representing their story. They planned to meld Amanda's engagement ring to her wedding ring in a few months to create one ring for her. She liked the idea of them being connected into one piece. After they exchanged rings, Lucas repeated the movie star kiss from the end of the second deployment when they were declared "husband and wife." Everyone clapped and cheered and then went to celebrate at The Keg.

They decided to play George Strait songs for the entire reception, and while they both tried to talk to everyone who came, they couldn't go a few songs without Lucas saying they had to dance to that particular song. The restaurant had cleared tables from one section for a dance floor. It was only when Lucas saw her parents dancing that he mentioned wishing his mother had chosen to come. His father, three aunts, two uncles, and four cousins had come from various places back East. Amanda had been most excited to meet the cousin who still lived in the Charleston area, although about an hour from the base. Thomas was engaged and would be getting married in September. Amanda was looking forward to going to the wedding with Lucas.

They took a limo to The Renaissance and had a wonderful night, but the next morning had them both tired and they started getting short with each other as they packed up and tried to get checked out so they could make it out the door by 8 a.m. They finally got the car loaded up at 8:10 a.m.

Amanda wanted them to take 10 minutes to eat breakfast there since she heard they had some of the best omelets in the city. Lucas finally agreed, but sat picking at a bagel and sipping coffee while she stood in the omelet line. She sat down and ate quickly when it was done, seeing that Lucas was agitated that they were running late. After all that, she barely tasted it. When it looked like she was almost done, Lucas stood up without a word and started getting them both coffee in to-go cups. She watched him and saw him put the lid on one black, but add two creamers and two sugars to the other one before putting the lid on it. She stood up as soon as she saw him do that, walked toward him, and hugged him from behind.

"What's that for?" Lucas said, surprised.

"That's because even when you're Mr. Grumpy Bear, you still make my coffee the way I like it. And that means you love me."

Lucas turned around and hugged her back and then gave her a long kiss.

"I do love you, even when we're 30 minutes late getting on the road," he said, but with a smile on his face. She picked up her coffee and he grabbed his and then grabbed her hand as they walked out the front door.

"Our adventure awaits," she declared.

CHAPTER

THIRTEEN

On Sunday, the first day of the drive, they didn't stop until almost midnight. They had 12-13 more hours on the road on Monday. Except for the drive over the mountains, they took turns driving and stopped every two to three hours to stretch their legs. Lucas took the drive to the base gate in Oklahoma, as Amanda didn't have a military identification card yet. He had told her they would get one this week when he had a lunch break. Amanda stayed in the car, barely able to keep her eyes open, while Lucas went in to find out what room they would be staying at on the base. It was in the same building, so they grabbed just what they needed for the night and went to their room and crashed. Lucas had to be at the in-processing briefing at 8 a.m. the next morning and would be back by 5 p.m. at the latest. They planned to wake up around 6 a.m. so they could unload the car and get some food for Amanda. The only place on the base she could buy food until she had an ID card was at Burger King or the food court, Lucas said. Her plan was to spend the day unpacking and making their room a little "homey" and calling her parents and Juliana with updates on their trip.

Amanda would also email Lucas' father to let him know they made it safely to Oklahoma. Amanda had been able to talk to him by herself for a bit at the rehearsal dinner. He seemed genuinely interested in what their plans were and talked about visiting them in South Carolina as he still had friends and coworkers there. He told Amanda that email was the best way to stay in touch with him. Amanda hoped to meet Lucas' mom sometime soon as they'd be just a long day's drive from where she lived in Florida. She had sent them a very nice, long handwritten letter wishing them the best and sharing some relationship advice along with a gift card to a bath and bedding store. They had requested that people consider giving them gift cards for the wedding since they didn't know what apartment or house they would live in when they got to South Carolina.

Amanda had just finished lunch when Lucas came back.

"They gave us an hour lunch break today. I grabbed a sandwich at the gas station and ate it on the drive over. Let's go try to get you an ID card today. You'll be able to get out of this room more."

They chatted about his morning on the way to the MPF office, which Lucas said stood for Military Personnel Flight. His class should only last six weeks if there were no delays in the flights. He said it didn't sound too hard. He'd have to study some each night, but they would be able to go out and explore the area some. The Fourth of July was a four-day weekend, so he thought they could spend that weekend in Oklahoma City.

At the MPF, they picked number 23 from the "Grab a Number" machine, and the sign flashed that they were currently on number 20. Lucas started filling out the paperwork, asking Amanda about her social security number and exact height and weight. Their number was called in just 10 minutes. Lucas seemed really surprised that they didn't need to wait long.

"I was hoping we'd get it done in time, but when I got my ID card, I had to wait two hours!"

They took Amanda's picture, had her sign the paperwork on a signature-catching machine, and then, after a few minutes, handed her a laminated card. The woman who was helping them was in uniform and had her hair back in a tight bun. She leaned over and explained to Amanda what everything on the card meant, both front and back. It had Lucas' information, where she was allowed to go, when it expired, her medical information, and a bar code for scanning.

"The scanning is mainly for the gate guards and the hospital to use to make sure your card is still current in the DEERS system," she said to Amanda. Then she turned to Lucas, "She is all set for everything except medical. You'll have to take her to the TRICARE office and get her put in their system in case she needs an appointment. You'll have to do that when you get to Charleston, too. Also, don't forget to get your orders amended. They can do that at the training squadron. You're not the first."

"Thank you," Lucas replied, and they got up to leave. Lucas looked at his watch. "You're good luck,

Amanda. Nothing is ever quick in the military, and here you got things done in 25 minutes."

When they got in the car, Amanda asked him about DEERS and TRICARE. He explained that TRICARE was their medical insurance company, and she would have to register at each military hospital they used. DEERS was a military-wide database that kept track of who was eligible for benefits and which ones.

"Nothing in the military works right if you're not in the right system," Lucas said. "I'll get my orders amended tomorrow and then once we stop by the hospital later this week, you'll be officially official."

Lucas took her back to the hotel, pointing out a few things on the base as they drove. He promised a full tour that night. He said would actually be able to get rides to training most days as some guys he knew from the first loadmaster school were here and staying in the same building, too. That way, Amanda could even go off base and see what there was to see.

Lucas was back at 4:30 and found the room all sorted out and Amanda asleep on the bed. He gently woke her up with a kiss and asked if she still wanted the tour and to go out to dinner. She yawned and said yes but said she hoped they could go to bed early that night.

He handed her a map of the base and a pen so she could make notes of places she might want to go. He went in a big circle and made sure she saw the fitness center, the hospital, the BX or base exchange with a food court, the commissary where she could buy groceries, the gas station, and the building he went to for training. He also took her by the flight line to show her the C-17s up close. She was in awe of how big the plane was.

"You'll be able to see them take off and land up close here. If you hear a big rumble, go outside and watch it take off. The tactical take-off is the best – it's what we can do if we have to get out of somewhere fast. You'll be able to wave to me when I go up," he said with a smile.

"It would be neat to fly in that, I would think," she said.

"Well, I don't know if they'll do it here, but at Charleston, I should be able to give you a tour inside of the plane and they'll probably have a spouses flight once a year where you'll get to be a passenger."

"Really?" she said, very excited about the possibility of taking a flight on a C-17.

"Really," he said. "Now, let's head to one of the best restaurants around here – A Little Off Base."

"What's it called?"

Lucas laughed. "That's the name and the location – A Little Off Base."

"Now, that's clever," she said.

Amanda got to meet several of Lucas' classmates at the restaurant. It seemed like almost everyone made it one of the first stops for dining at Altus. There were three other wives there and one girlfriend. They all exchanged information. The girlfriend and two wives had work-from-home jobs, so they were busy most days, but the other wife, Stephanie, was a teacher, too, and since they didn't have kids or pets, she was able to come stay with her husband. They were stationed in Alaska and Stephanie also didn't want to be there by herself for most of the summer. Amanda and Stephanie planned to go to the gym together the next morning and see what classes were offered. Stephanie mentioned the base also offered some day trips for shopping and sightseeing twice a month, which could be fun to go on together.

Between doing things with Stephanie a few times a week, finishing up her paperwork for her teaching license in South Carolina, applying for jobs, reading, updating her lesson plans, and doing some online house hunting, the days passed by quickly. They ate out most nights or stayed in and ate leftovers or pizza. Their room only had a small refrigerator and a microwave, so they couldn't cook full meals. They spent Saturdays sightseeing and Sundays studying. Amanda helped quiz Lucas when she could. She loved knowing when he was going up in the air, but she started to notice that she would feel relieved when the plane landed. She wasn't actively worrying when he was up in the air, but she must be in the back of her mind.

After their weekend in Oklahoma City, there was a week full of thunderstorms and tornado warnings. The class was a week behind after that. When it was time for Amanda to fly back to Washington, she didn't know if she'd see Lucas soon in Washington or later in South Carolina. She truly hoped he'd make it to go on the long drive with her, but she wouldn't know until just a couple days beforehand.

She had two weeks to pack up her apartment and get the contents in a U-Haul when she got back. Her parents picked her up at the airport and took her to dinner before taking her home. While they had been to Oklahoma before she was born, they had only driven through it on their way to other places on trips with her. They shared stories about places they had all seen now. Her mom offered to help her pack during the week if she wanted help, and Amanda told her she'd let her know.

Amanda called Juliana just to let her know she was back in Washington, but the call went to voicemail. Amanda knew Juliana and Brian were getting more serious as they were going out to explore Chicago together almost every night. Although they worked for the same company, they worked on different floors and different projects, which Juliana was actually happy about. She wanted to see Brian a lot, but not all the time. Amanda secretly hoped there would be another wedding soon for her and Lucas to go to together.

Despite being tired, Amanda had trouble falling asleep that night until she pulled out a T-shirt of Lucas' she had tucked away in her luggage and stuffed a pillow in it. She wasn't used to sleeping alone anymore. She knew she'd have to figure out something because as soon as they got settled in Charleston, he would be back on the road again.

Amanda started packing by tackling one room at a time. She bought a lot of boxes and packing tape and, at Lucas' insistence, had been careful to tuck the receipts away somewhere safe. He said he had filed to do a partial DITY move when he told her about the move. Her confused look must have been clear to him because he then explained that DITY was do-it-yourself, and the government had three ways to move people's belongings: the government could do it all, the person could do it all and file for reimbursement, or it could be partially government-moved and partially person-moved and the person could be reimbursed a certain amount depending on the weight and what the government's cost was for the move. It sounded complicated, but

Lucas was sure they would be under the weight allowance since he wasn't moving any furniture other than a bed and desk and Amanda just had a couch, kitchen table, bed, and desk. The government would do Lucas' move and since they didn't get married until after Lucas was packed up and they had to add Amanda to the moving orders after-the-fact, they would move her belongings and then get reimbursed for it. Amanda kept an envelope in her purse to tuck away receipts for everything related to the move, including gas receipts for their drive across the country. It sounded complicated to Amanda, but she trusted Lucas knew the system better than she did.

Amanda emptied out the small coat closet first and decided to use that for the items she wanted to keep with her in the car. She would have a suitcase for two weeks' worth of clothes, and she wanted to keep important papers and her laptop with her. She also planned to put a tub with all her teaching supplies and lessons in the car. If she did get a job, she would have only two weeks to get ready from when they got to Charleston. She actually had a couple phone interviews next week lined up. She didn't want to have to dig for her supplies in case they hadn't completely moved into a place by then.

She made plans with Jodie and a few friends from school and work to meet up with and say goodbye that week. Lucas called every night, and they talked for at least an hour each night. He was hopeful they would finish up by the next Wednesday and then he would be back to help her load the U-Haul and start driving Saturday. But, on Monday, his flight got cancelled due to a maintenance issue, and on Tuesday it was cancelled for weather when a small tornado actually touched down three miles from the base. He finally made it up in the air Wednesday and passed his last test Thursday. He would out-process Friday morning and fly to Washington that afternoon. He had even found someone from class who would take his car to Charleston for him for a small fee.

Amanda's parents helped her load the truck that day and clean the apartment. She had planned to spend the night at her parents' house, but with Lucas coming in, she booked a hotel in downtown Tacoma. Unlike the last road trip, they only had to drive six to eight hours a day and planned on a few stops to spend a day sightseeing. They didn't have to leave at any certain time the next day to start the trip, and her parents suggested they plan to leave by 10 a.m. at the latest so they would at least get out of Washington State the first day. Amanda thought it was a good idea and was glad they were going with them. She was also so glad her parents and Lucas got along so well.

She picked Lucas up at the airport that night and surprised him with the night in a hotel. She slept soundly that night with Lucas beside her.

CHAPTER

FOURTEEN

Amanda couldn't wait until she could sleep in her own bed once they got settled in Charleston. It had been a great trip, and they had taken turns riding with different people throughout the trip "so they couldn't get tired of each other," her father said. About halfway through the trip, they even split up for dinner, parking at a mall and planning to meet back at the vehicles two hours later. The time they each had alone definitely went a long way to helping keep any arguments at bay. At breakfast each day at the hotels, they would review the plan for the next three days and plan exactly where to stop that night. They hadn't done that the first two days, and it led to some worrisome moments later in the afternoons when no one had cell phone service and they had lost sight of each other. They had managed to find each other at rest stops both days, and then they decided to plan a stopping point in case it happened again.

They got to Charleston in mid-afternoon after only 10 days on the road and unloaded the U-Haul into a storage unit near the base. They got Lucas's truck, returned the U-Haul, and took Amanda's parents to the RV rental location. After saying goodbye, Lucas and Amanda went to check in on base. The room was just about the same as the one in Oklahoma. They both sighed at the same time as they saw there was no stove again. Lucas promised they could visit the housing office the next day.

"How would you feel about living in a house on base?" Lucas asked.

"What would that be like?"

"I think we would get a two-bedroom house and it would probably be a duplex or quadplex, so the neighbors would be close. I think we may not have to wait so long if we move into a house on base first. It could take us a while to find something off base to rent that we liked."

"It would probably be convenient, and I know we both wanted to feel settled fairly soon. Can we look at it first?"

"Yes. If they have anything available, they could show us it tomorrow."

"Guess it's worth seeing what they have," she yawned. "I need to send three emails about the job interviews before we go to bed tonight. Hopefully I can line those up in the next day or two, as well."

"Why don't you do that and I'll go find us some dinner and bring it back? I'm up for going to bed early tonight, too. I'm glad I fly everywhere for my job. Driving is tiring."

The Ring

Amanda's brain felt like it was swirling every day their first week in Charleston. There was so much to do and so many decisions to make. They were shown and offered two houses when they went to the housing office. Lucas had been right on both the duplex and the quadplex. The duplex was newer and empty, so they decided to take it and they had an appointment to get the keys and do a walk-through inspection in two days on Friday. Lucas lined up the delivery of his belongings, and over the weekend they would use his truck to move her belongings out of storage. Amanda had two job interviews Thursday afternoon and one Friday morning before their housing appointment. Two were at a high school and were a 30-minute commute from the base. The district right outside of the base had an opening for a middle school teacher, and she really wanted that job the most. She felt they really liked the fact that she was a military spouse as there would be a lot of military "brats" in her classes. The principal even said she liked that Amanda had already taught military kids in Washington.

They got as settled as they could over the weekend, which included two trips to Walmart on Saturday and four trips on Sunday to get food, toiletries, curtains, curtain rods, towels, extension cords, laundry detergent, and other odds and ends off a continually updated list left on the kitchen counter. Lucas would start in-processing on the base on Monday, and his belongings would be delivered on Wednesday, so Amanda would have to be home all that day. If she got one of the jobs, the before-school training would start on Thursday. Everything was at least lining up just right.

On Monday afternoon, Amanda got a call from the Charleston School District offering her the middle school job. She was so excited. She called Lucas right away and got his voicemail. She then called her mom and Juliana and talked to them both for 30 minutes each. She barely heard the door open as she was hanging up with Juliana. Lucas came in with two dozen roses, a bag of caramel Ghirardelli chocolates, and moose track ice cream.

"Congratulations, my smart wife!" he said and handed her the presents. "Sorry I missed your call, but as soon as I got your voicemail, I knew we'd have to celebrate tonight. I asked around and found out the best Greek restaurant around here and I'd like to take you there for dinner. If it's good, it could be our new Phyllos."

Amanda wrapped her arms around him and thanked him with a kiss.

Lucas didn't have to leave on his first trip until October, so they had some time to get settled into their house and explore the area a little. Right before he left for Australia, he told Amanda that Terri and Will were moving to Charleston in early December and would be in the same squadron. Amanda was excited about the idea of having someone she knew there. One couple from Altus and two guys from the class were at Charleston, but they lived off base and were in different squadrons. Amanda hadn't made it to any of the spouse events yet, but had gotten to know a few teachers from school, two of whom had husbands who worked on the base as civilians and three whose husbands were in the military, but not in any of the flying squadrons. She had worried about finding friends moving to a new location, but it seemed those attached to the military made every effort to include newcomers, which made it easy for Amanda to feel welcomed.

Lucas was gone for both Thanksgiving and Christmas that year. There was a lottery system for who got leave, but you weren't allowed to participate the first year there. There was a squadron Thanksgiving feast potluck a week before at the base housing's clubhouse. It was the day before Lucas was heading out, so they only went for a little bit to have a Thanksgiving experience together at least. Amanda ended up spending Thanksgiving with some single coworkers from school who were all going to Denny's for dinner and then for drinks at a piano bar. Amanda skipped the bar, feeling really out of sorts that day spending a holiday without any family around.

Amanda didn't find out about Christmas until her last day of teaching before the holiday break when she came home and found Lucas packing. Although she knew it was a possibility that he would be gone, she was hoping he would be able to stay. She started to cry. Lucas held her until she was ready to talk.

"I'm sorry, Amanda. I wish I didn't have to leave you for another holiday. It's Europe, though, so I can get a big stash of all the good chocolate to bring home with me."

"I'd rather have you than chocolate."

"I know. Hey, why don't we look at you going home for Christmas?"

"That would be nice. I know my parents are staying home this year. They were invited to Uncle Eddie and Aunt Vicky's for Christmas dinner. The plane ticket wouldn't be cheap, though."

"We'll figure that part out. You shouldn't be alone on Christmas."

"I guess I didn't think about how much lonelier I'd be with you gone all the time away from my family and hometown."

He kissed her forehead. "I know, sweetheart, but it's only a few years and then we can talk about whether I stay in or get out and go back to Washington."

"It would be nice to see you every day for a while, whether here or in Washington."

"I love you, Amanda."

"Love you, too."

Amanda ended up going to Washington for a week for Christmas. She stayed with her parents, and her mom took her shopping and to the Nutcracker ballet in Seattle. They wrapped presents, delivered cookies to neighbors, and watched a different Christmas movie every night. Amanda knew her parents were excited to have her home, but they could tell she was missing Lucas. Her mom did a good job of trying to keep Amanda busy and distracted.

Lucas had mailed a few small presents to her parents' house for her to open on Christmas. She had snuck two into his suitcase, too. Amanda smiled at the thought of them both trying to be sneaky about making sure they both had presents from each other. While Amanda was opening a bracelet from Lucas, she heard her phone ring. It was a long-distance number she didn't know, but she had the feeling she should answer it.

"Hello?" she said. There was a small pause.

"Amanda, it's Lucas. Merry Christmas!"

"Merry Christmas! Thank you for the presents. How are you calling me?"

"I love my new wallet and watch. Thank you. I'm getting to call you from the plane. We're flying back across the ocean right now. I should be home the same day you get home."

"That's great news! How can you call me from the plane?"

"It's something with HF and HAM radios. I can explain it better in person. They don't let us do it often because it's mainly for emergencies. But they sometimes make holiday exceptions."

"It's so good to hear your voice!"

"Yours, too. My time is about up, love. I'll see you in a few days."

"Love you!"

"Love you, too!"

Her parents were amazed that Lucas had been able to call from the plane. It definitely helped lift Amanda's spirits. It was one of the first things she told her aunt and uncle when they went to their house that afternoon. She played a lot with Alice and her new toys while her uncle and dad watched football and her mom and aunt finished up the dinner preparations. They ate early while Alice took a nap, so Vicky could enjoy a meal without getting up at all. Amanda did a lot of talking, telling them about South Carolina and her new job.

Amanda flew home two days later and got back to their house right as Lucas called to say they had landed and he would be home in an hour or two after checking a few things in the office. He had a whole week off after that trip, and they were able to spend New Year's Eve together in downtown Charleston.

"I have great news," Lucas said after going back to work in the new year over dinner. "I asked for leave the week you have spring break, and it got approved. Want to go to Hawaii then?"

"Yes! I thought we wouldn't be able to go until summer. Finally, a honeymoon!"

Amanda took two days off herself so they would have a day to pack and unpack on either end. They still had the money they had saved up for the honeymoon, so it wouldn't affect their finances, especially with the military discounts Lucas could get. The other teachers were quite jealous when they found out how she was going to spend her spring break. A few who had been to Hawaii gave her tips, and the ones with children told her to enjoy doing such things before they came along. They were spending their spring break at zoos and children's museums.

Juliana was thrilled that Lucas was able to get the time off to take Amanda on a make-up honeymoon. She told Amanda she was afraid it would end up never happening because of his military commitments. Then, she shared news of her own.

"I'm glad you called because I was going to call you today. Brian asked me to marry him last night!"

"Congratulations, Juliana! Tell me all the details. You said yes, right?"

Juliana laughed. "Yes, I said, 'Yes!'"

Brian had taken her to their favorite Italian restaurant and then they walked around downtown. They ended up at the library, which had a big lawn in the front of it with street lamps lining the sidewalk around the lawn. It was always lit up. Brian had led them to the middle of the lawn to "enjoy the view" and then he got down on one knee and proposed. It was one of Juliana's favorite parts of the city, so it was the perfect place for Brian to ask. They were going to have the wedding in Chicago, and it would probably be in the summer or fall.

Amanda shared the news with Lucas, and they pulled out some wine to toast Brian and Juliana.

"To happiness in love," Lucas said.

"To happiness in love," Amanda replied. "Just like us."

About a month after coming home from Hawaii, Amanda was looking at her calendar and realized she was four days late. She was taking birth control pills and was always very good about it, but she had heard there were always the rare cases it didn't work. Lucas and Amanda both wanted to have kids eventually, but they wanted to wait until Lucas was done with his degree and could possibly find a job, military or not, that had him home more often than gone. She decided to pick up a pregnancy test, tell Lucas at dinner, and then they could discuss it and he could be there when she took the test the next morning.

"Wait, what?" Lucas said, putting his fork full of food back down on his plate.

"I know, but all I can say is it's not a for-sure thing. I can take the test in the morning."

"Amanda, this would be crazy."

"It would, but I think we'd be fine. It's not the timing we'd want, but we could handle it. A lot of people do."

"You're right. You know most people in flying squadrons have girls, right?"

"Really? Any reason for that?"

"They say fliers and scuba divers have girls because the male swimmers are weaker than the female ones and they die off up in the altitude or below in the pressure."

"A girl ...," Amanda was already imagining a little girl who looked like her and Lucas. Lucas got up and came over and knelt by her chair.

"I'm ready if you are," he said, taking her hand. "Let's see what the morning holds."

Neither of them said much during dinner, each lost in thought about the possibility of a "honeymoon" baby coming in nine months. They decided to go to bed early, thinking it would help the morning come sooner.

It turned out Amanda didn't need the test in the morning. Her period had started. They both felt a little bit sad and relieved. Now they both had the idea of a baby in their heads, but they both agreed their original plan of waiting was the best – at least that's what they told each other that morning before they both headed off to work.

CHAPTER FIFTEEN

The rest of the school year passed quickly, and Lucas and Amanda planned to explore the area as much as possible during the summer. They went to Lucas' cousin's wedding in mid-June and then took a long weekend to visit the Outer Banks. Lucas was home for the Fourth of July, so they took a week and went to Washington, D.C., to watch the fireworks. There was a comfortableness developing that they had never experienced before. They were both getting used to the comings and goings of Lucas and life in South Carolina. Amanda went to most of the spouse events and saw Terri at most of them, but made sure she had some friends from work who were outside of the military lifestyle. Even though Amanda and Terri got along well, Lucas explained to Amanda that as an officer's wife, Terri would probably hang out with other officer wives more than enlisted wives. Amanda had noticed there were usually two different groups at most of the events, but didn't realize it had to do with military rank. As Lucas explained to her, it became clear but it really made no sense to her. Lucas agreed with her that it shouldn't really matter, and it really shouldn't matter in a flying squadron when the crew all depended on each other's skills and experience, not rank.

Amanda got to host the spouses August book club meeting on Tuesday before she and Lucas left for Chicago for Juliana's wedding. Lucas had started volunteering at a local soup kitchen when he was in town and met some guys through that who played poker together once a month. It turned out that poker night was book club night this month. Lucas usually stayed out until at least midnight on poker night, but this time he came home around 9 p.m. right as the book club members were leaving. He quickly said hi to Amanda and then went right to their office in the second bedroom. They had a futon couch in there for when guests stayed the night, which wasn't often. Amanda said goodnight to the last two guests and then went to see what was going on with Lucas.

"Is everything okay?" she asked as she opened the door. He was sitting on the couch with his head in his hands. He looked up at her, and she saw sadness in his eyes.

"I just got alerted. Apparently, Rick came down with appendicitis and is having surgery, so I have to go in his place tomorrow night. My leave for this weekend is cancelled."

"I have to go to Juliana's wedding by myself?"

"I'm sorry, Amanda. We can get a plane ticket if you don't want to drive by yourself. That's what I came in here to do, but then I started dreading having to tell you. Juliana's going to kill me ..."

Amanda sat down beside him and put an arm around him. "It stinks, but it's not your fault. Juliana will understand because I do. I was looking forward to experiencing this weekend with you, but when the military calls ..."

"Sometimes I wonder if you're for real. When Pete called me, he told me he was glad it was me and not him because his wife would have thrown something at him if she had to reschedule her spa weekend for what would be the fourth time."

Amanda sighed. "It's not easy for us, but at least we don't have kids and no sitters like Pete and Arielle. That spa weekend was his five-year anniversary present to her. She got it three months ago, and it still hasn't worked out for her to use it. Not a lot of sitters will handle their 2-year-old twins more than once."

"Well, they are all redheads – fiery hair, fiery spirit."

"I think I would like to fly to Chicago if I'm going by myself. I can fly out Friday and come back Monday. You don't mind if I go see the Sears Tower without you?"

"I don't mind. I'll start looking for tickets. I don't need to pack until tomorrow. Can you throw our laundry in the washer while you call Juliana, please?"

"Sure."

Amanda called Juliana with the news, but Amanda could sense she was in full pre-wedding mode. She asked right away if Amanda would still be there on the same days, and Amanda said yes. She would actually have left Sunday afternoon after the farewell brunch with Lucas, but now would stay the night on Sunday and leave Monday. She could call the hotel and change that herself, though, so Juliana wouldn't have to deal with it. Juliana would be on her way to Napa Sunday afternoon anyway.

Juliana told her she couldn't change the catering numbers now, so if Amanda wanted to bring someone else, she could. She told Juliana she probably wouldn't, but would let her know if she did.

Amanda was the maid of honor and wanted to make things as easy for Juliana as possible so she could enjoy the wedding. She had taken a quick trip to Chicago over Memorial Day weekend to go dress shopping with Juliana. She got to meet some of Juliana's new friends and got to meet Brian. Amanda had been surprised to find he was an inch shorter than Juliana and blond, since she usually dated the tall, dark, and handsome type. Brian was great, and seeing him and Juliana together left Amanda with no doubts that Juliana had found a good man.

Amanda helped Lucas pack on Wednesday, and they went out to dinner before he headed to work. His flight didn't leave until almost midnight. After they said goodbye, Amanda watched TV until she was really tired and then finally went to bed around 1 a.m. She always had trouble sleeping the first night Lucas left on any trip. Her phone rang around 5 a.m. It was Lucas. He should still be over the ocean.

"We had to turn around, so I'll be coming home to get some rest before we try again tonight," he said, yawning when he was done.

"Oh no! I'm glad you got back okay."

"The pilot thinks it's just a software glitch, but it wasn't worth the risk."

"I'm glad. Come on home. I'll work on some professional development webinars so the house will be quiet and you can sleep."

"Thanks, Amanda. I'll see you soon. Love you."

"Love you, too."

Lucas slept for seven hours and then was up again to try leaving again. The night was a repeat of the previous night except Amanda had run out and gotten Chinese food so they could eat at home. They split sesame chicken and beef and broccoli and each had an egg roll. Lucas always got some egg drop soup, too, as it was one of his favorite dishes.

Amanda started packing a few things after Lucas left. Her flight wasn't until 1 p.m., so she had plenty of time in the morning to finish up, and she was more tired than the previous night. The phone rang again at 5 a.m. It was Lucas.

"Amanda, my trip is cancelled. The plane needs maintenance work. I'm going to hang out at the office to get my leave re-approved. I get to go with you to Chicago after all!"

"Really?" Amanda felt fully awake at the thought of Lucas actually being able to go with her.

"I know! Can you get the plane ticket for me? And pack up my suitcase? I'll be home as soon as I can."

"I can do that. What a wonderful surprise!"

"Sometimes things work out," Lucas said. "See you soon. Love you!"

"Love you, too!"

Lucas ended up being the coffee and food runner for the bridal party during the rehearsal and before the wedding. He delivered their orders with a smile on his face, and Amanda always rewarded him with a kiss. The mood between them felt like a heightened romance as they recalled their wedding and quick honeymoon and then the real honeymoon in Hawaii. They danced together a lot during the reception.

"I'm so glad I got to be here with you," Lucas said. "No one should be alone at a wedding."

"It definitely wouldn't have been as much fun without a dance partner," she replied. "Plus, I probably would have fallen asleep during the wedding due to lack of caffeine."

They laughed and got a piece of wedding cake to share. Juliana and Brian made the rounds to see everyone before they left for their hotel. About half of the guests had already left as it was getting late. The photographer was nearby and got a picture of the four of them together and grabbed a few shots of just Amanda and Lucas when Juliana and Brian moved on. Amanda made a mental note to get some copies from Juliana in a month or so.

Juliana had been a very nice bride and had only requested the color of her bridesmaids' dresses and not the style. The deep burgundy color looked great on Amanda, and she loved the dress she picked out. Lucas had a matching tie and the picture was sure to be a great one of them. She considered getting it on a large canvas to add to their mantel, which had their wedding picture, a picture from their engagement, the caricature from the Washington State Fair, and a souvenir photo from Hawaii. Lucas' voice interrupted her thoughts.

"One last dance, please, my beautiful wife?"

"Of course, my handsome husband." They danced, and for a few minutes, Amanda's world was just Lucas and her and the music.

They slept in the next day and then went to a celebration brunch for the wedding party and immediate family to send Juliana and Brian off on their honeymoon. Afterward, Amanda and Lucas headed for the Sears Tower together. It was a beautiful day with the sun out and just a slight breeze. When they reached the top, they both just stared at the city for a while. Lucas reached for Amanda's hand.

"Amanda, I've been thinking a lot this summer about us having children," he said, still looking out at the city.

Amanda turned to stare at him, and he finally looked at her.

"I think I wouldn't mind us trying sooner than we've planned," he continued. "What do you think?"

"Oh, Lucas, I've been thinking the same thing all summer, too. I haven't been able to stop thinking about the possibility of a baby since back in February."

Lucas kissed her, and they both smiled big.

"Let's see about the adventure they call parenting," he said.

"Anything we do is fine by me – as long as we do it together," she said.

When they got home the next night, Amanda and Lucas had a toast as Amanda threw away her birth control pills. She told him she had heard it sometimes takes a few months to get pregnant once you stop taking the pill, but she had known some women from the spouses groups who had gotten pregnant right away. They both hoped for Amanda to be pregnant by Christmas.

Christmas came and went, and Amanda still wasn't pregnant. She spent all of the Christmas break reading about fertility and was going to start taking ovulation tests and tracking when they made love. They had to be more intentional, she guessed.

She had gotten recommendations of some books and web sites from a coworker at work who had just announced her pregnancy and mentioned it took them a year of trying. It didn't help that Lucas was gone a lot still. He was home for Christmas Eve and Christmas this year, and they just had a small celebration at home. Amanda's parents were going to come, but a massive snowstorm in the Midwest on the day they were supposed to leave – December 23 – had a ripple effect and their flight was rescheduled for December 26. They still came, and Amanda showed them around the area. They had their own small Christmas together, just a bit late. She hid all the infertility books in her room while her parents were there, but her mother could sense something was wrong and asked her about it one day while her father was in the office checking his email.

"Is everything really okay, Amanda? You seem a little down. Is it just Lucas being gone?" her mom asked.

"Well, that doesn't help, but it's not just that." Amanda hadn't told anyone but her coworker about their difficulty getting pregnant. She needed another person to talk to about it. "We're trying to get pregnant, and it's just not happening."

"It can take a while for some people. How long now?"

"Almost six months."

"Oh, it took me that long to get pregnant with you, so you're probably right on track. And Lucas can't have been home the perfect time every month, so it may only really be about three months or so."

"That's true. I didn't think to ask how long it took you. That would have been smart. I'm sure genes play a role in all this."

"They do. But, if it takes much longer, you probably should see a doctor and make sure you're both as fertile as you should be."

"That's not a bad idea. I'll ask Lucas about that next week."

"As excited as I'll be to be a grandma, remember, there's no rush to these things. You and Lucas are still new to this marriage thing."

Her dad came back in to the living room, and they started talking about their plans for the day. Amanda was thinking about how she could discreetly make an appointment for Lucas and herself. The problem with doing anything at the OB/GYN department at the base hospital was the gossip chain. Amanda still couldn't believe how much the women in the squadron talked about other wives and their personal business. At first, Amanda had been a little bummed that no one from their squadron lived on their street, but once she heard people discussing other families' comings and goings and what was put on the curb for trash, Amanda was glad to have some distance from the spouses in the squadron. Maybe they could find a doctor off-base.

Lucas actually thought it was a great idea that they get their fertility checked out. He figured out a way they could do it on base for now. He would make an appointment through flight medicine, and she would go to OB/GYN and tell anyone she saw that it was just her annual checkup. They both made appointments in January, and had the results back in early February. They were both normal. The doctor had told Amanda that while the military required couples try for a full year, documenting each month, before they were referred to an infertility specialist, they had just changed to require nine months of documentation out of 18 months for those on flying jobs since they were traveling a lot.

It took Amanda and Lucas 14 months to get nine months of documentation, and then they were referred to an infertility specialist. The doctor discovered that only one of Amanda's ovaries was actually releasing eggs, so they didn't even have a chance every month, just when the one good ovary released an egg. He recommended IVF but sent them home to look over all their options, which included considering adoption. They were both quiet on the drive home from the appointment, but once Amanda spread all the paperwork over the dining table at home, she started to cry. Lucas came up beside her and wrapped an arm around her.

"I didn't think it would be this hard. I didn't know I could want something so badly, either," she whispered to him.

"I thought it would be easy, too. I'm sorry, Amanda." He took her completely into his arms and let her cry. When she finally looked up, she could see his eyes were wet, too.

"I have an idea," Lucas said. "Let's maybe put all the baby stuff on hold for the next three months until school is done and then I'll put in for a week of leave and we can go on a trip to start our summer. When we get back we can look through all these papers and options and research and then make a decision. But, I think we need a break."

"Lucas, that is a wonderful idea. I think it would do me a lot of good to get my mind off of all this for a while."

"Sounds like a plan. Now, how about we go out to dinner and talk about where we want to go this summer."

"I would like that."

"I'll put this stuff away in the office and then we can head out." Amanda kissed him and went to check her makeup before they headed out. Her heart felt lighter than it had in months. She had been so focused on trying to make a baby come into their lives – it was definitely time for a break.

Amanda and Lucas decided to go to Florida for a week after spending a few months living more like they had when they first got married. All the books, ovulation kits, pregnancy tests, and charts had all been tucked away in a printer paper box, along with the paperwork from the doctor. Lucas had put it up on the shelf in the office closet. They spent most of their vacation at the beach but decided to spend a day at Disneyworld toward the end of the week, to celebrate their second wedding anniversary a few days late. Amanda enjoyed showing Lucas around since her parents took her once in middle school. They briefly talked about the baby issue on the drive home, planning to sit down the following Saturday and start looking at their options. Lucas needed to do some currency flights that week and Amanda was going to finish cleaning up and organizing her classroom. She also planned to start tidying up their office at home. Juliana and Brian were going to visit for two days around the Fourth of July before heading to some training for work in Washington, D.C., for a week. Amanda hoped Lucas would be in town for the visit so she and Juliana could spend a day by themselves without feeling guilty for leaving Brian alone. Juliana assured Amanda that Brian would actually love a day by himself to just read and write. He was working on writing a motivational book geared toward college students.

Lucas came home that Wednesday with flowers, ice cream, chocolate, and gummy worms – all of Amanda's favorite things. By the look on his face, the gifts weren't for a celebration, though, but for consolation. She guessed another trip or training was coming up, possibly a long one.

"Let me guess," she said. "You won't be here for the Fourth of July?"

"Actually, I should be home for that."

"So, then is there training coming up in Oklahoma?"

"No, Amanda, it's actually worse than that. It's another deployment."

Amanda turned around and walked into the living room and sat down. She felt furious. Lucas followed right behind her, put the gifts on the coffee table, and sat next to her. She knew in her head there would be a deployment in the next year or two, but her heart was hoping that somehow the possibility would go away. Lucas grabbed both her hands in his.

"We had the quarterly commander's call today, and they made the announcement. I'm still surprised there were no rumors of it in the squadron beforehand. We leave in mid-September, and it's another six-month one."

Amanda put her head on his shoulder and sighed. Her anger quickly turned to sadness. "Every time I feel like I get used to you being around, you have to leave."

They were both quiet for a few minutes, and Amanda finally lifted up her head. "I'm going to miss you, Lucas."

"I'm going to miss you, too. I think this one is going to be the hardest. The longer we're married, the more I want to stay home and just have a normal life that's more predictable day-to-day."

"Can you imagine having a job where you were home every night and every weekend?"

"Actually, I can and I do. At least when I'm back from this deployment, we can start talking about options for our future. It's only one year until I get my degree and two years until my enlistment is up. I'll start looking into what cross-training options there are while I'm deployed so we can know what other jobs I could do if I stayed in the military."

"Do you think you'd be able to walk away from the military completely?"

"If it meant being with you more, yes, Amanda, I would walk away in a heartbeat. I only get this one life to live with you."

"Sometimes I wonder if it's so easy for us because we don't see each other every day. You aren't around enough for me to truly drive you crazy."

"I'm up for you driving me crazy," he said, and they laughed. "But, seriously, we will look at all the options when I get back. We don't have to stick this military thing out until the end."

"Maybe we should wait and review the baby options when you get back, too. Just leave that box up on the shelf. We can plan our whole future out once you're back safely."

"That sounds like a good idea, Amanda," he said. "Oh, they did mention that everyone should plan to take two weeks of leave sometime between now and the deployment. I put us down for the beginning of August so we're back before you need to start work."

"Back from where?"

"You'll see. I have a great idea, but I need to do a little more research before I tell you. I want us to do a fun trip before I leave, though."

"I'm always up for traveling with you." Amanda was smiling, despite the bad news of the deployment. They had a bright future ahead, and a trip to end the summer would be fun.

CHAPTER SIXTEEN

Amanda got to see Lucas more that summer than any other time since she'd met him. Their squadron was put at the bottom of the mission-tasking list as they got ready for the deployment. He had one trip to Europe in July and one in late August. It was great to have him home for the Fourth of July weekend. Amanda and Juliana got to spend a day out shopping while Lucas took Brian on a tour of the base and planes. They went downtown to watch the fireworks display and then slept in the next day before doing some of the area's tourist attractions that Juliana and Brian had never seen. Juliana and Amanda decided Amanda would go to Chicago after Christmas for a week so they could celebrate New Year's Eve together. Lucas thought it was a great idea. He had been suggesting Amanda plan some trips to visit people while he was deployed to help pass the time. She would go back to Washington for Christmas, too.

Juliana gave Amanda a big hug before they left and reminded her she was allowed to call anytime, especially when Lucas was gone. Amanda was so glad she had been able to see Juliana. It definitely helped lift her spirits.

Lucas told her they needed to go to a will appointment the week after the Fourth of July. It was part of the pre-deployment checklist, and Lucas wanted to get them done earlier as appointments would get booked up as the deployment was closer. It gave Amanda an odd feeling to be making wills at their age. They had no children and no huge assets. He reminded her that if something happened to both of them, they wanted to make sure they were buried together and that certain items went back to certain parents. Amanda conceded it was a good reason to have a will. She honestly didn't care what happened to most of her things if something were to happen to her. It should all go to Lucas. As she started thinking about what she would do if something happened to Lucas, she stopped herself quickly. She didn't even want to think about something happening to him. It couldn't.

The will appointment actually wasn't too bad. Lucas printed out a worksheet with questions that they filled out the night before, and everything seemed very straightforward. She still felt odd during the whole appointment and only felt better once they got home and put the wills into the small safe tucked away in the back of their closet.

"Now that that's done, I'm free from deployment readiness until the few weeks before the deployment. So, I'm ready to let you in on where we're going in a month."

"Where?" she asked eagerly. She asked him every few days for weeks, and he wouldn't even give her a clue.

"We're going to ...," he pulled out a pamphlet from his pocket and handed it to her.

"Alaskan Cruises," Amanda read. "Alaska? On a cruise? Yes!" She jumped up and then hugged him tightly. "That was my favorite place we went to growing up!"

"I love hearing your stories about it, and I thought it was time to see it myself, and not just for a few hours stop at Elmendorf for fuel," he said. "We'll fly up to Seattle and spend one night with your parents before getting on the cruise. We'll actually fly back from Alaska so that we can spend a few days exploring on our own."

"This is going to be so much fun! This is definitely a trip of a lifetime!" Amanda started talking about all the places they should make sure to see and what clothing they should pack. She'd never been on a cruise and neither had Lucas, but they could figure that out together. The best part of going there, though, was that it would be distracting enough to take her mind off Lucas' impending departure. She had worried that it would put a damper on their pre-deployment vacation. But, Alaska was a true adventure, and they could pretend for two weeks like they would never be apart.

Amanda and Lucas had a great time on their cruise after spending some time with her parents. The weather was clear almost every day, and they took pictures together at almost every landmark. Amanda planned to make a photo book of the trip and she'd add the best picture to their collection on the mantel. The cruise docked at Sitka, and they took a train to Anchorage after going out on a fishing charter. They both caught some salmon and halibut and had their fish sent home on ice, completely processed, to arrive the same day they got home. Amanda told Lucas she couldn't promise there would be any left after he got back home. He joked he would just label a few packages as spinach and she wouldn't touch them.

The tour stops only took them as far as Anchorage, so they rented a car and spent a few days making their way to Denali. One of the cruise workers had given a speech at a dinner about the correct Alaskan lingo to use for a few things so they didn't stick out like tourists too much. The biggest one, he said, was not to call the tallest mountain Mt. McKinley, but Denali. True Alaskans held it as a deep affront that their mountain was named after someone who had never even visited the state but was from Ohio. Denali was what the natives called it, and that was its true name.

They spent one day visiting Hatcher Pass and the Iditarod Museum in Wasilla. They spent a night in Talkeetna and then spent a whole day at Denali before flying home from Fairbanks. As they waited to board their flight, Lucas caught Amanda staring at him.

"What?" he asked. "Is something wrong?"

"No, I just wish we didn't have to head back. I don't want you to leave me."

He wrapped an arm around her, and she laid her head on his shoulder. They stayed like that until it was time to board. They would have just a few weeks at home and then Lucas would deploy.

Those few weeks went by quicker than either Amanda or Lucas thought they would. Amanda went back to teaching, and Lucas had appointments, training, flights, and packing. They went to the family pre-deployment briefing together, and Amanda was the one who reached out to the girlfriends so they could be included in the spouse activities. The woman who had run the book club had PCS'd that summer to Oklahoma, so Amanda was taking over the role. She still felt weird using some of the military lingo – PCS was short for permanent change of station, which really meant a move. Amanda thought it was ironic that they used the word permanent in an acronym that meant a military move. There seemed to be nothing permanent about the military – except change.

Lucas had a full three days off before the deployment, and Amanda took time off from work that Friday and Monday. Even though they were scheduled to report to leave at 8 a.m. on Monday, Amanda knew she wouldn't want to go into work that day. The spouses were going to have a kickoff dinner that night with various countdown crafts to make for both the children and adults. Amanda was going to make a chalkboard countdown in the shape of a heart. They were offering journals, paper chains, memory jars, and scrapbooks. Some of the spouses had even gotten matching T-shirts that said "Another Deployment" on the front and "We're In It Together" on the back with the squadron logo. They were going to do a second order since several spouses wanted one after seeing them. Amanda was ordering a red one. If there was anything good about a deployment, it was the camaraderie between the spouses and families who were left behind.

Lucas and Amanda didn't leave the house until Sunday night that last weekend. Lucas helped Amanda clean and organize, and Amanda helped Lucas pack his last-minute things. Lucas made sure as much around the house was taken care of as possible and the cars were tuned up before he left. He was trying to prevent the deployment curse, but Amanda knew it was bound to happen. Within a few days or weeks of the deployment, each household seemed to have at least three things go wrong in rapid succession. Terri told Amanda that the last time Will deployed, the furnace stopped working, the kitchen sink started leaking, and the garage door broke – all within the same week. At least since they lived on base, Amanda could call the housing office and a maintenance worker would come fix whatever was broken. The only things she was responsible for were the cars, washer and dryer, and lawn.

Three teenage boys whose own fathers were deploying with the squadron would take care of the lawn. It was going to be one boy's Eagle Scout project. There had been a front-page article in the weekly base newspaper about their project. Amanda planned to take the article in to the principal since the boys went to the school where she taught, although she hadn't had them in any of her classes.

Amanda had finally gotten the photo book and canvas print in the mail from their Alaska trip that Saturday. Before going out to dinner on Sunday, they spent some time looking through the book, and Lucas helped her hang the canvas on a spot on the wall beside their wedding picture. The best picture had been the one of the two of them in front of the Alaskan Railroad train. Another cruise passenger had taken it of them. They had their arms around each other and were smiling. The sun was behind the train, and the colors were vibrant. After he hung it, they stood back and looked at the snapshots from highlights of their life together so far.

"Which one is your favorite?" she asked Lucas.

"The engagement one," he said quickly. "I love that I completely surprised you."

"I love the wedding one, of course, but I love how happy we are in the Alaska one."

"I think we'll get happier in each photo we add," he said. "A whole lifetime of happiness is ahead."

Neither of them spoke much Sunday night or Monday morning. They had swapped journals at dinner. Amanda had prepped them with the dates, but they each filled them out with notes for each other to read, and there was space for each to jot down what happened each day. They had both liked the journals last time, but they had decided not to do daily, weekly, or monthly notes as they would be able to stay in better contact this time. Video chatting was more mainstream, and Lucas would be able to do it from his room and not just at the base's setup.

The mood at base ops was very different than the homecomings. Each couple or family was in their own separate small group, and people were whispering, hugging, kissing, and crying. Some of the moms with children were already leaving after saying goodbye, not wanting to prolong the event for the children's sake. Amanda and Lucas sat down on the floor side-by-side and held hands. She leaned her head on his shoulder. They didn't talk until it was time for Lucas to leave. They stood up and hugged each other tightly. Amanda felt tears well up in her eyes.

"Come back to me soon, Lucas," she whispered.

"I will. I'm going to miss you terribly," he said. He pulled away to give her a long kiss. "I love you, Amanda."

"I love you, too." After one more hug and one more kiss, Lucas picked up his bags and walked toward the double glass doors. She stood still and watched him. He turned back and looked at her and smiled. She waved and he waved back. Then, he was gone.

The first week without Lucas went by slowly, especially since Amanda had trouble falling asleep most nights. Then, her life starting falling into a routine. Lucas was helping more with office work, so he was able to email her every day. They were going to try to video chat once a week on the weekends, and they talked for almost an hour that first Saturday. The time difference had Lucas waking up early and Amanda staying up late for the video chat to work. The next weekend, Amanda was hosting book club on Saturday night, so they chatted Friday instead. Amanda really liked being in touch with Lucas more often. It was almost better than when he was on trips.

The third week was the one where the deployment curse happened. Amanda had to take Lucas' car to work since her engine light came on. Her neighbor, Linda, picked her up from the mechanic and took her home. The water heater stopped working the next day, and it took two days before someone from housing could fix it. Amanda wondered what the third thing would be, and she found out when she went to video chat with Lucas on Saturday. Her laptop wouldn't boot up. Luckily, Lucas had installed a server that automatically backed up all her files, so she hadn't lost anything, but she was disappointed that she wouldn't be able to see Lucas that night. She sent him an email through her phone to tell him what happened, and about 20 minutes later, her phone rang with an odd long-distance number. She smiled, knowing it was Lucas. He had bought a prepaid international phone card so that they could talk on the phone for emergencies or in cases like this one.

"Hi, honey," she said. There was a slight pause before she heard his voice.

"Hello! Sorry about your laptop," he said.

"I'll have to see if I can get a deal through work or maybe just wait until Black Friday," she said. There was another pause. She realized this must be part of international calling.

"Don't wait. I want to be able to see you next weekend!" She could hear the smile in his voice.

"That has been really nice."

They spent the rest of the time talking about the car repair bill and how he was glad the water heater got fixed relatively quickly. He said another guy in the squadron's family had to wait a whole week to get theirs fixed off base.

Lucas said he was going to train for another race while he was there. A few of the guys were planning on doing a Tough Mudder in April, and he was going to join them. He thought he might do especially well since he was able to stay on the ground more this deployment. She said she'd cheer him on, but was going to stick to her spin and Zumba classes. They said their goodbyes after 30 minutes, not wanting to use up all the time on the phone card.

"Amanda, make sure you're taking care of yourself. I love you!"

"Love you, too!"

Amanda thought about his goodbye for a few minutes after she hung up. It was different from what he usually said, and she wondered if she'd said anything to make him think she wasn't taking care of herself. She'd have to make a point of sharing with him how she was doing that by going to the gym and doing at least one spouse event a week and doing a night out with teacher friends once a month. She knew he didn't want her sitting at home every night while he was gone.

CHAPTER

SEVENTEEN

After a long day giving most of her students a test and trying to grade most of them once she got home, Amanda finally grabbed her journal and a glass of wine and sat to watch one TV show while writing to Lucas before heading to bed. She had written a few sentences when the doorbell rang. She looked at the time on her phone and guessed it was probably a neighbor needing something, although 9:19 p.m. was a little late.

Amanda went to the door and peeked through the peephole. There were three men in dress uniform, the squadron commander's wife, and Terri. Amanda felt her heart drop into her stomach. Her first thought was a small hope that they had the wrong house. Lucas wasn't flying until later that week. Nothing could have happened to him.

She slowly forced her hand to grab the doorknob and unlock the door. She took a step back as she opened the door.

"Mrs. Weston?" the man closest to the door asked. She gasped and her hand flew to her mouth. She sank to the ground and started crying. She could feel it – Lucas was gone.

She woke up the next morning and for a second was blissfully unaware of how her life had changed. Then, she realized she was on the couch and could sense there were other people in the house. She kept her eyes closed as she remembered how she had only stopped crying long enough for them to tell her how Lucas had died. He had been on a run and when he went near one of the gates, there had been an attack on it and shrapnel had struck Lucas in the leg, shoulder, and head. The attack lasted mere minutes, but by the time someone was able to check on Lucas, he was already gone. She had curled up into a ball on the couch facing away from them and just cried. Terri had tucked tissues on the top of the couch. The chaplain tried to talk to her twice, but she couldn't find the words to respond. All she could do was cry until she finally fell asleep. Now, she was crying again but was able to sit up and see who had stayed with her. It wasn't the chaplain, but the other military man and Bethanne, the squadron commander's wife, who had stayed the night with her. They were whispering in the kitchen, and Amanda could smell coffee. She grabbed a tissue and attempted to wipe the tears off her face, but they kept coming. She got up and went to get some coffee and face the people who were in her house. They both stopped talking as soon as Amanda appeared. Bethanne walked over quickly and put an arm around Amanda.

"Do you feel like eating? Want any coffee or juice?" she asked.

"Coffee, please," Amanda said as Bethanne guided her to the kitchen table to sit. There was a plate of muffins on the table, which made Amanda look around the rest of the kitchen. There was a plate of cookies on the counter and a bowl of fruit. An entire coffee service had been set up by her coffeemaker and she somehow knew the refrigerator was stocked, including with juice that she and Lucas never bought, but these well-meaning people thought she might need. Amanda knew when people didn't know what else to do, they tried to provide food. Everyone had to eat at some point, but Amanda wasn't hungry at all.

Bethanne put the coffee down in front of her, along with the service tray that had cream, sugar, and various kinds of fake sugar. Even though Amanda usually put a lot of cream and sugar in her coffee, she decided to try and drink it black that morning. She didn't know why except that maybe she felt she didn't deserve comfort if she was alive and Lucas was dead. After she took a few small sips, Bethanne and the man sat down at the table with her.

"Mrs. Weston, my name is Capt. John Stegner. I am going to be your casualty assistance representative, which means I am here to help you during the next few months as you make decisions about your survivor benefits and Staff Sgt. Weston's estate. I am truly sorry for your loss, and your country is grateful for your husband's sacrifice."

Amanda just stared at him. The words seemed pathetic compared to how Amanda's heart was breaking, but his eyes conveyed that he felt her hurt to a degree.

"I really am sorry, Mrs. Weston. I knew Lucas, and he was a good loadmaster and a good man. A lot of people are going to miss him." She saw the tears in his eyes and reached out to grab his hand. The other hand went over her eyes as she started sobbing again. She pulled her hand back from the captain and grabbed a tissue box that seemed to have just appeared on the table. They let her cry for a few minutes before Bethanne spoke up.

"Amanda, I know today is going to be a rough day. There are many of us who are here for you and we're going to help you as much as you'll let us. Would you be up for a few people visiting today? Mainly just your close friends?"

Amanda looked at Bethanne and nodded.

"Terri and I, along with Mrs. Stegner, are going to take turns throughout the next few days staying here with you and helping keep the flow of traffic minimal. If you ever don't want to see someone or want to take a break, all you have to say is, 'Is that an airplane I hear?' and we'll clear everyone out for you."

"I will be here a few hours each day," Capt. Stegner said. "We'll cover a few topics each day, but I do have three questions I need to ask you today."

Amanda steeled herself for some tough questions. She knew she'd have to make decisions about his funeral and then she knew she couldn't stay on base for long, but she didn't know how long. She was starting to feel a little relieved that there was someone here to help her.

"The first question is if you would like us to notify the rest of the family or if you would like to." Amanda realized she should have already thought to call Lucas' parents and her own, but she had been so shocked by the news she had only thought of herself.

"I will call them. I should do that now," Amanda started to get up to find her phone.

"Let me ask you the other questions real quick and then we can do that. I'll stay while you call in case you want to hand me the phone for any details you have a hard time telling.

"The other two questions are if you would like to go to Dover to meet the remains when he comes back and if you want to speak to the media about Lucas at all."

"Oh, yes, I need to go meet the plane," she said and looked at Bethanne. "I should do that, right?"

Bethanne nodded her head yes in a gentle way.

"Have any reporters called?" she asked Capt. Stegner.

"Two have, but we haven't released the name yet, so they don't know very much."

"I'd rather not talk to them," she said.

"I'd do the same," Bethanne whispered.

"Most people don't want to talk to them, from what I hear," Capt. Stegner said. "Let's make those calls."

Bethanne produced Amanda's phone before Amanda could get up from her seat. She called Lucas' dad first, and he picked up after four rings. He was quiet and then started asking questions about what would happen next and after Amanda said "I don't know" a few times in a row, Capt. Stegner took the phone and explained he or Amanda would be in touch once decisions were made. Lucas' mom and her mom had both started crying right away, and Amanda started crying more along with them. Capt. Stegner calmly talked to

Lucas' mom and told her they would be in touch and even made sure she would call a friend to come over right after they hung up. She asked her own Mom to get Dad on the line to talk to Capt. Stegner and then she got up and went back to the couch and lay down. She had tried to avoid looking at the pictures on the mantel, but had seen the one from Alaska right before she closed her eyes. She just wanted to sleep and wake up to find out this was just a nightmare. But, first, she called Juliana, and she cried again with her best friend crying along with her.

She woke up to the smell of bread. No one was in the living room with her, but she could hear someone in the kitchen. She got up to find out who it was and get some water. It was a spouse from the squadron who she had seen at events but hadn't gotten to know very well.

"Hi, Amanda," she said, and Amanda could tell she was usually a very happy person and she was trying to sound less happy for Amanda's sake. "I'm Candace Stegner. Bethanne asked me to come over for a few hours. I hope you don't mind that I was baking some bread."

"It smells good." Amanda stood there for a minute and then walked over to get a bottle of water from the refrigerator. She remembered her guess from earlier that it was fully stocked and she was right. There was milk, juice, wine, sandwiches, a fruit tray, a vegetable tray, and at least four casserole cartons. She closed the door and drank half of the water. Her stomach rumbled loud enough for Candace to hear.

"Are there still muffins around?" Amanda asked.

"Over on the table." Amanda grabbed a banana off the counter and sat down at the table. She ate half of the banana and only three bites of the muffin before her appetite went away. Candace must have noticed she stopped eating because she washed the flour off her hands and walked over to the table. She put her hand on Amanda's shoulder.

"There is no right or wrong way to feel right now. I won't pretend I know what you're going through, but I will listen to you if you want to talk and do anything I can to help you. I have thought many times what it would be to be in your shoes when John was late coming home from a flight. All of us wives want to help you in any way we can. Your friends really want to see you today if you feel up for it."

Amanda was grateful for the honesty in her words. She didn't know what anyone could do to help her right now, but it was true that as a military spouse, they had all thought about this possibility and hoped their doorbell would never ring.

"Let me shower and then they can come over," Amanda said.

"Take your time," Candace said. "And, Amanda, I really truly am sorry for your loss."

The next few days were a blur with visitors coming and going. She sat with Capt. Stegner for about two hours during lunch each day to make decisions and go over her "benefits." She felt really odd hearing that word because no benefit would truly be a benefit without Lucas around. John had agreed with her, but they couldn't think of a better word to call it. Her parents and Lucas' parents were going to meet her next week in Washington, D.C., to meet the plane carrying his casket and then for a full military funeral at Arlington. Amanda and Lucas had wanted to be buried next to each other after living full, long lives, but Amanda knew that he wouldn't mind being buried in Arlington since his death was tied to his service to his country.

Amanda thought she had spent all her tears when she cried over his casket after it was taken off the plane. Her mother finally came to move her away from the casket, and she realized all the military present were standing at attention and would stay that way until she was willing to let Lucas' casket be loaded into the waiting car. His parents both went up to the casket when she stepped back and they each put a hand on the casket while holding hands.

There were more people at the funeral than Amanda had expected. She softly cried through the whole ceremony, clutching the flag they gave her in Lucas' honor to her chest. Her father kept an arm around her shoulders. Amanda was glad for her parents' presence as so many people Lucas had worked with through the years came by afterwards to tell her how sorry they were and what Lucas meant to them. Juliana and Brian had come out for the funeral. They and Capt. Stegner took turns taking care of Amanda, her parents, and Lucas' parents. Juliana was going to fly home with Amanda later the next day and stay with her for a few days. Juliana would help her with some personal decisions, like whether she should go back to work and whether she should stay in South Carolina, head back to Washington, or move somewhere new. Amanda's parents and Lucas' parents all had to get back to work. Amanda hadn't thought about her job until day three after, which is now how she kept track of the days. She found out Bethanne called right away the next morning and had spoken to the principal. Mr. Valencia had been in the Army himself. He only told the staff that Amanda had a family emergency and then procured a long-term substitute for her class. When the news went public, he held a staff meeting to tell everyone in person. Flowers and cards from fellow teachers started arriving later that day.

On Day 16 after, Amanda and Juliana went to a coffee shop downtown to try and get a plan together for Amanda. They had been mulling over all her options the past two days in the house, and they both thought a change of scenery might help. Juliana was leaving the next day, and Amanda knew if she didn't decide with Juliana there, she would put it off for several more weeks. Making decisions about her future without Lucas made things feel more real and she missed him terribly. Amanda still woke up in the morning thinking Lucas was just on a deployment and then each morning her hope died again as she looked over and saw the flag in its case on their dresser. Other than the flag, it was hard to believe he was gone when there were still so many reminders of him around the house.

Juliana pulled out the notebook they had been using to make lists of ideas the last few days after they settled themselves at a table with coffees and scones. The leaves on the trees outside were bright red.

"Do you want to go back to work?" Juliana asked.

"I think I still want to teach, but I'm not sure I could handle going back to Hamilton. Too many people there would give me those pity looks every day," Amanda said. She had gone back after school one day to give an outline of the upcoming syllabus to the substitute, and every time she ran into someone, it felt awkward.

"So, you could teach here, but at a different district?"

"I could, but I have to move somewhere within a year or less since I live on the base."

"If you could work and live anywhere, where would you want to go?"

Amanda closed her eyes, and the first place that came to mind was Tacoma, but a tear slipped from her eye as she saw Lucas in every place she remembered from there.

"I think I'd like to go back to Washington, but not Tacoma. Maybe I could live in Seattle or even Spokane."

"Spokane? All the way across the state?"

"I would still be able to see my parents for holidays, but no one would know me or my story. If I have to start over, it might as well be a completely fresh start."

"Well, when you put it like that, it could be a good spot. What about Chicago?"

"I do think I'd like to be closer to home than that, even though it would be fun to live near you and Brian."

"When would you want to move out there?"

"Maybe in January. I'm going to go home for Thanksgiving and Christmas. In between, I can start sorting and packing and looking for a place to live and apply for jobs."

"Is your teaching license still good in Washington?"

"I think so, but I'll check on that. I guess I won't plan to work until the next school year, but if I get settled early enough, I can always do some substitute teaching."

Juliana jotted down the plan so they could tell Capt. Stegner about it when they went to his house for dinner that night. Candace invited her over once a week, not wanting her to be alone. John called Amanda every afternoon to check on her, too. It actually seemed like the squadron spouses were all picking a day to check on her as hardly a day went by without someone knocking on her door with food or a restaurant gift card.

CHAPTER

EIGHTEEN

She waited until the beginning of December to start packing. She knew she wanted to sort through Lucas' things first so she wouldn't have to do that when she moved into her apartment in Spokane. She wanted his mementos tucked into boxes and labeled so she could put them in the back of a closet and pull them out when she wanted to remember. It took her three days, two bottles of wine, and four boxes of tissues to sort through Lucas' clothing, photos, jewelry, military mementos, and other personal items. She had started with the box of items they had brought back from his deployment, along with his duffel bag. She kept one flight suit and all his military patches and pins but put the rest of his uniforms in the donation pile. She kept five T-shirts from locations they had visited together, along with a few of his white undershirts that still smelled like him. She added his watch, high school class ring, and dog tags to her own jewelry box but hid them away in the bottom drawer.

She was going to organize the office next, but after only an hour of looking through papers and files with Lucas' handwriting and stumbling upon a paper that had a sticky note that said "Amanda, Just sign on the back at the bottom. Love, Lucas," Amanda left the room and shut the door. She was emotionally drained. She hadn't answered the door since she started packing, not really wanting to see anyone while she sorted through their memories. She did answer her phone but only for family, Juliana, and Capt. Stegner. On her second day of packing, Capt. Stegner asked why she wasn't answering her door. She explained what she was doing, and he said he'd pass the word along but that Bethanne might want to put eyes on her soon. She'd call first, though. He also said Candace would come over anytime if she did want company. Amanda thanked him but knew she wouldn't want company.

Amanda went to the living room and started throwing out old magazines. She disconnected the PlayStation and added it and all the games to the donation pile in the garage. She saw the uniforms in the pile and looked around the garage, not knowing what tools she should keep and what ones she would never need. She went back to the living room and found herself staring at the mantel at their wedding picture. She crumpled to the floor and started sobbing. Why wasn't he here? How was she supposed to do this all on her own? Why her? Why them? If only he hadn't gone running. If only he hadn't been deployed. If only she had kept herself from falling in love with a military man. But how could she not fall in love with Lucas? How could Lucas really be gone?

At first the thoughts were just in her head, and then she started getting mad. She started yelling out her frustration with her situation to the walls. When she was done yelling, she felt a little better, but still mad. She started tackling the house again. She took all the pictures off the mantel and placed them face down on the coffee table. She unhooked the rest of the wires for the TV, DVD player, and stereo, complaining that now her father would have to help her set up her television since her husband wouldn't be there. In her fury, she took a trash can to the bathroom and threw away all of Lucas' toiletries and then went to the kitchen and tossed the leftover junk foods that were his favorite.

"If you're going to be gone, then be gone," she shouted, getting worked up again. A glass fell out of the cabinet she opened to look for the German coffee he liked but was too dark for her. It was a glass from a German restaurant that he brought back from his first trip after they were married. She found herself on the floor again crying for a long time before she could get up and sweep up the glass. She took the trash bag to the garage and put it on the opposite end of the donation pile. She decided to let the movers pack up the entire garage and she would ask her dad to help sort through the tools later. Her parents had offered several times for her to come live with them until she felt settled. She wished she felt she could to that, but she wanted a fresh start. She and Lucas wanted to have a baby, and now that child would never come to be. Amanda found herself crying again, and she decided she was done for the day. She had one more day before the movers came, and she still needed to sort through the kitchen a bit more and tackle the office.

She ate a bowl of cereal and had a glass of wine before heading to bed.

Just as she was leaving the kitchen, she felt a sharp pain in her foot. She knew it was a sliver of glass from earlier. She felt herself getting angry again. She looked at her foot and didn't see any glass sticking out. She felt the area and could feel that it was a very small piece of glass. There was no way she would be able to get it out by herself. She limped to the bedroom and started yelling at Lucas again.

"You should be here to help me. You should be sorting the office and making the moving appointments and getting the tweezers to get this glass out of my foot! Why aren't you here? Why, Lucas?" There was no answer, of course.

"Fine. If you aren't going to be here, then just go!" She took her wedding ring off her finger and threw it into the closet where all his belongings were boxed up and then flopped onto the bed and cried herself to sleep, again.

The next morning, even though she told herself to wait, she spent an hour desperately searching for the ring in the closet before giving up. She had so much to do that day, she would have to look for the ring again when everything else was done. Her thumb kept brushing the empty space on her finger. Why should she even wear a ring anymore, she thought? Lucas was gone and, therefore, they were no longer married. She was no longer married. She was a widow. She was a war widow. She looked down at her finger and wondered how long it would take for the indent to disappear. If it did by the time school started in August, she might not even have to tell anyone in Spokane about her sad past. She would truly have a clean slate.

She had just finished the kitchen when Capt. Stegner called to check on her. He mentioned that Candace would be over in the morning and Bethanne in the afternoon to help her keep an eye on the movers. They were going to take all of her food items and donate them to a food bank for her, too. She was hoping to load up her car in the morning before the movers came with the items she wanted to take with her on her trip across the country. Everyone she had told that she was going to drive by herself to Washington had offered to go with her, but she really wanted the time to clear her head and prepare for her new life in Spokane. She was going to spend a week just exploring the area and looking at apartments before spending Christmas with her parents. Then, she would head back and get settled and apply for jobs.

She opened the office door and steeled herself to go through the files. There were four drawers in the filing cabinet, and Amanda needed to decide if each paper should be thrown away, shredded, packed by the movers, or taken with her. She got through each drawer by rewarding herself with a half glass of wine when she finished each one. There was a large pile to be shredded, but she knew she could ask Candace to work on it the next morning. She opened the closet door and saw more file boxes and sighed. Then, she saw the white box on the top shelf and closed the door back up. There would be no baby now. She decided to back up her laptop and then move the box to the trash pile.

She hadn't turned on the laptop since the day they came by with the news and she felt a slight shock when she saw the background photo of their engagement photo. She quickly hit the back up button on the top of the screen. She was going to close the lid to put the laptop to sleep during the back up but noticed her calendar button at the bottom. She clicked on it and made it full screen. She wondered if she had missed anything important in the past few weeks. She scrolled through and saw a dental appointment, a staff meeting, several spouses get-togethers, and then she saw the green square at the top of today's date, which meant she should be having her period. But she wasn't. In fact, she started to think about when she'd last had one. She had never gone back on the pill. She and Lucas were so sure they wouldn't be able to get pregnant without help, so she hadn't worried about anything happening. She'd had a period right before they went on the cruise but couldn't remember having one since. No, there was no way, she thought. It must be all the stress she'd been experiencing. And she hadn't been eating well. She stood up and opened the closet door back up and got the white box down from the shelf. She took a deep breath, opened it, and quickly moved things around to look for the pregnancy tests. She grabbed one and then quickly put the lid on the box. She started breathing again, but it was shallow breaths. She took the test, put it on the bathroom sink and then sat down on the floor with her back against the wall. She closed her eyes and thought over and over and over again, "I cannot be pregnant. I cannot be pregnant. I cannot be pregnant."

She didn't let another thought enter her head until she felt enough time had passed to check the test. She stood up, but she couldn't will herself to step forward and look. She was barely able to face living without Lucas by herself. How would she be able to do it with a child? She chided herself, saying the odds of her actually being pregnant were so low that she should just look and chalk it all up to stress. She could see her doctor up in Washington next week, and he could confirm that stress could affect her in that way. She smiled, telling herself she was being overly dramatic, and stepped forward to look. She picked it up and saw two lines. She dropped it like it was burning her and realized the noise she was hearing was her own voice. "Nooooo!"

She ran to the bedroom and curled up into a ball on the bed. She cried and screamed on an off for a long time. Why now? She didn't want to be pregnant when she didn't have a husband. She didn't want to be a single mother. She did not want to be pregnant at all. Maybe she wasn't. Maybe it was a false positive.

At first, she wanted to call her mom and Juliana and ask them what they should do, but then she realized she didn't want anyone to know. Who would believe a war widow was pregnant with her dead husband's child? Of course her parents and Juliana would believe her, but the rest of the world would think differently. She couldn't let the other spouses know. She'd wait and see a doctor in Spokane to make truly sure and then talk to someone. Yes, there was no sense changing any of her plans until she knew for sure from a doctor. With that resolve, Amanda got up and went to finish sorting the office. She wouldn't let herself think about anything other than the task at hand.

Candace was surprised at how much Amanda had done to prepare for the movers when she arrived at 7 a.m. with bagels and coffee. Amanda had barely slept the night before, finding her mind wandering every time she tried to lie down, so she kept herself busy. She got the shredding done and bagged up all the pantry items. She had even loaded up her car and taken the donation items to the local thrift shop late in the evening and then loaded the trash can when she got home, burying the pregnancy test deep in the bags. She even sorted through the garage before finally feeling like she would fall asleep quickly. She was going to have Candace and Bethanne take the tools she didn't want to their husbands.

Packing day went by quickly with various people from the squadron coming by to say goodbye throughout the day. Amanda gave everyone a few minutes but then told them that she was tired and needed to get back to the movers. It was true, but she also didn't want to chit chat. It took almost all her energy to keep her mind off her possible pregnancy. Over and over she said in her head, "No, I can't be pregnant. No, I can't be pregnant."

It wasn't until she did a final walkthrough with the housing office representative and Capt. Stegner at the end of the day and they were in the bedroom when she remembered her lost wedding ring. She looked all over the closet but didn't see it. She told the balding man who was checking items off a list and Capt. Stegner what had happened, and they promised they would keep an eye out for it. She hoped it was packed up somewhere. Maybe a mover had found it and put it with her jewelry. She sighed. She wanted the ring back, but as she looked down at her finger, she knew she couldn't wear it. She was all by herself now.

CHAPTER

NINETEEN

She thought she could make it all the way to Spokane before seeing a doctor, but when she saw the sign for the pregnancy center in Missouri that offered free pregnancy tests and checkups, she found herself taking the exit and heading to the building. The billboard said turn left at Wendy's and it would be straight ahead. She parked and walked in to the building quickly, knowing that if she stopped to think about it, she would never go in. She had to know after spending so many days in the car going back and forth about what her future would look like with or without a baby. She tried to just stick with facts after having to pull off the road in Tennessee. She thought about naming the baby Lucas if it was a boy and started sobbing. Thinking about a part of Lucas living on and about a baby never meeting his father had overwhelmed her, and she couldn't hold back the tears. It almost felt as if she was losing him all over again. Once she regained control of her emotions and got back on the road, she kept the music loud to drown out most of her thoughts.

She walked into the center, noting the sign was very nondescript, calling it a Women's Resource Clinic. She was glad she could go somewhere away from a military base. If she had to get the test done while at Charleston, she knew there was a good chance someone would see her and there would be gossip. There were a few women she would miss from the spouses group and from work, but she was really glad she was going to get a fresh start. Maybe. She knew she couldn't live in Spokane by herself with a baby. Maybe there would just be no baby.

The waiting room was empty, and Amanda went up to the reception desk. No one was there, but there was a sign-in sheet. She wrote her name and sat down. The TV was playing "Sleepless in Seattle." Amanda saw some magazines on the table beside her, but leaned her head back and closed her eyes and tried to think about nothing.

"Amanda?" she heard after just a few minutes. She opened her eyes and looked toward the reception desk. "I'm sorry to keep you waiting. We were having a quick staff meeting. You can follow me back."

Amanda followed her, and they went into a room that had four comfortable armchairs. The woman gestured for Amanda to sit.

"I'm Leesa, and I've been working here for seven years. We'll start with a few details about your situation and then see how best we can help you."

Amanda gripped her hands together and said the words out loud for the first time. "I think I might be pregnant." Then the tears started to fall. Leesa moved her chair right next to Amanda and handed her a tissue and then put her hand on Amanda's shoulder. She let Amanda cry for a while before speaking again.

"Whatever your situation is, we can find a way to help you. I think we should start with a pregnancy test first, though."

"I took one, and it was positive."

"We like to make sure, and if it is positive, we can do an ultrasound to see how far along you are. Do you have any idea when you might have gotten pregnant?"

"It had to have been in August before my husband left."

"I'm sorry to hear that." Amanda looked at her and realized Leesa thought her husband had walked out on her.

"No, he left for a deployment and then ..." Amanda started crying again. "He died over there." Since telling her and Lucas' parents and Juliana, she hadn't had to tell anyone about Lucas dying. The whole base knew her story from other people or the news. She saw true sympathy in Leesa's eyes.

"My nephew died on a deployment five years ago," Leesa said and put her hand on top of Amanda's hands. "I'm so sorry for your loss."

The pregnancy test was positive, and they moved to a different room for the ultrasound. Amanda heard the heartbeat and saw the baby moving around. Leesa said she was probably about 20 weeks pregnant and was due in early May. A doctor would be able to confirm exact dates for her and could tell if the baby was a boy or a girl in a few weeks.

After the ultrasound, they went back to the first room, and Leesa handed her some of the ultrasound pictures and a printout of the clinic's results from the pregnancy test and ultrasound.

"I guess this is real," Amanda said staring at the photos. "Lucas and I made a baby, and I didn't even know it. He didn't even know it." Amanda was sad, but she wasn't crying. While it wasn't what she wanted, now that she knew for sure she was pregnant, she could feel a little hope well up in her heart. Instead of a fresh start, she would just start another chapter in her and Lucas' love story – one that included raising their child. She thanked Leesa and promised to stay in touch. She only wanted to go to one place now – home. She had to tell her parents and figure out a way ahead that would include a baby.

She only answered one phone call a day and made only one for the rest of the trip. She always answered when Capt. Stegner called around 1 p.m. to check on her and see where she was that day. Those calls were always pretty short. She always called her mom at night to let her know where she stopped. That night, Amanda did her best to keep her voice normal as she told her mom she had decided to head to Tacoma first instead of Spokane. She said she just wanted to not sleep in a hotel room for a while, but she knew her mom could tell something was going on with her. Amanda guessed her mom would chalk it up to grief, though. Her news wasn't something that she wanted to share over the phone. She had to tell her parents in person. And she couldn't tell Juliana or Capt. Stegner until after she told her parents.

She arrived at her parents' house a few days later just before dinner. Her mom had chili waiting in the crockpot. Amanda told them about some of the interesting things she had seen on the drive while they ate and then explained to them the real reason for her change in plans, only shedding a few tears. Her dad's eyes grew a bit wide, but her mom gasped and hugged her.

"Oh, Amanda, this is such a blessing. A part of Lucas will live on."

"That part is wonderful, isn't it? But it's also going to be very hard."

"We will help you," her dad said firmly. "You are definitely not alone. You are welcome to live here as long as you want, and, well, we were going to tell you some news when you came home in a few weeks, too."

"We've decided to retire this summer," her mom said. "Our plans are just to stay in this house and travel when we want. We'll both stay on the list for subbing, but we can choose the classes we want to take."

"Wow! Congratulations!"

"That also means we can help take care of the baby if you want to work," her mom said.

Amanda was quiet for a minute. She didn't know yet what she wanted to do.

"I haven't even thought that far ahead," Amanda said.

"We'll figure it all out in time," her mom said.

The next day, Amanda called Juliana to tell her the news. Juliana was quiet and then asked Amanda how she felt about it. Amanda explained her mixed emotions, but how she had felt that bit of hope when she could see the baby and knew Lucas would always be with her. Juliana congratulated her and had some excitement in her voice. Amanda thought it was nice that Juliana wanted to see how Amanda was feeling before giving her own reaction.

"I'm going to tell you something that you can't tell your parents yet. I'm eight weeks pregnant!"

"What? No way?"

"Yep, we're waiting a few more weeks to tell people but how amazing is it that we both get to do the pregnancy thing together."

Amanda laughed. She hadn't laughed in weeks.

"Oh, what was that? I think ... Juliana, I think I just felt the baby kick!"

"He must like to hear your laugh."

"He, huh?"

"Of course, because I'm already pretty sure I've got a girl and so you need to have a boy and then we'll be in-laws in about 28 years."

Amanda laughed again. So did Juliana. It felt like she hadn't laughed in a very long time, and it felt good.

Over the next few weeks, Amanda dealt with all the new details in her life. She found a doctor and got a complete checkup. She was in good health, and the baby was as big as it should be. She needed to take some prenatal vitamins to get her iron levels up a little more. She decided to not find out if the baby was a boy or girl. The surprise would be a small, last gift from Lucas. She knew the baby would be named after him either way – Lucy if she was a girl.

She also told Capt. Stegner, who was working on changing her move from Spokane to Tacoma. She was going to have her stuff moved to a storage unit until she found a place long term. She was working with a realtor to find a small three-bedroom house and was hoping to end up not too far from her parents. Capt. Stegner was going to fly out in February to do a final check on her and transfer her to a local casualty assistance representative. He said she'd be in good hands with Capt. Thomas. Capt. Stegner knew him from pilot training. They wouldn't be able to add the baby to any paperwork until the baby was born and she had a birth certificate. She and the baby were both covered by health insurance through the military, and while she could opt to have her baby on the base, she decided to use the off-base network and see a doctor she knew. That way the baby would be born in the same hospital where Amanda was born.

In April, Amanda finally moved into a house that was only a 10-minute drive from her parents' house. It was tan with dark blue shutters, and everything was on one floor. It had three bedrooms and a fenced in yard. The previous owners even left a playset with a slide and two swings. The house had a large front porch and an attached garage. There was even air conditioning for the few days in the summer they might need it. Juliana and Brian flew out for a long weekend to help her move in. Her dad borrowed a truck from someone at work. The guys delivered all the boxes, while the ladies unpacked and put things where they belonged – and took lots of pregnancy breaks. The previous owners had left all the appliances as a free bonus, and Amanda knew the realtor had told them a war widow was buying the house. At first, she didn't like the idea because it seemed like pity. Then she realized how much time, hassle, and money they were saving her and they probably just wanted to help somehow – just like she would. She made sure to write them a thoughtful thank you note for her realtor to deliver. Once all the boxes were in the garage, the guys started setting up the big furniture, which included a new crib in the bedroom closest to the master bedroom. The walls had all been freshly painted a nice light brown color a few months before when the owners put the house on the market. Amanda was just going to use wall stickers to decorate the nursery, although she still hadn't picked out a theme. That was hard to do without knowing whether the baby was a boy or a girl.

The house was just about set by the time Juliana and Brian had to head back home. They went out to dinner at Phyllos on their last night there to celebrate. When the meal was served, Brian raised his glass for a toast.

"To Lucas," he said. "May he always be with us and may we love Amanda in his place."

Amanda faintly smiled and felt her eyes welling up with tears as she participated in the toast. She was glad she was not alone to face this future without Lucas.

Amanda decided to spend the first year getting settled and spending time with her baby before thinking about going back to work. She met with a financial planner from the base several times to review how best to invest and use the insurance money from the military. It was a big help to have some financial security for a while. She would have to go back to work at some point, but if she was careful, she and the baby could get along comfortably on a teacher's salary and interest payments. She had learned the baby would have his or her own benefits from the military that would help with education and insurance.

She spent the last few weeks before her due date making sure the house was clean and in order, napping, and started going through the boxes with Lucas' personal belongings. She wanted to put some of his things in the baby's room, and she was hoping it would help her pick out a theme. Sometimes she was still mad at him for not being there, but that was mostly when she wasn't feeling well or when it got hard to do things being so pregnant, like tying her shoes. Lucas would have already had a theme picked out, and he probably would have painted the baby's room.

She had only put one picture of them up, and it was on the office desk. It was the picture of them in front of the Alaska Railroad train. It was a memory tied to the baby, so she could look at it and just get teary, but not fall apart. When she had opened the box that had all the photos of them from the mantel, the rest of the photos left her crying for almost three hours. She had put that box in the office/guest room closet, along with the photo album from Alaska when she came across it. Someday, she'd be able to look at their pictures again.

Amanda realized as she looked at the assortment of T-shirts she'd kept and the items she had saved that there was a definite theme to Lucas' life, and the theme for the baby's room became clear – travel. She would get a large wall sticker of the earth and stickers that looked like various passport stamps. She had a boomerang from Australia, a pair of chopsticks from Japan, a tea tin from England, and a tiny gondola from Italy. Lucas had tried to get a souvenir from every country he visited in case he never got the chance to go back. She called her mom that night to tell her, and her mom was thrilled.

They spent every night that week shopping for decorations, and her parents helped her put everything in order over the weekend. They even found a globe lamp and airplane night lights. As if the baby knew Amanda was finally ready, she went into labor the next day.

CHAPTER

TWENTY

N o one had told her there was a possibility
the baby wouldn't come home with her.
Her labor lasted 16 hours. Amanda got an
epidural and experienced very little pain once the
epidural started working. Her mother was in the
delivery room with her, and Juliana called every
hour to check on her.

"It's a girl!" they said and showed Amanda her
little face before taking her to the exam table. They
were just supposed to check her over and wipe her
off and give her back to Amanda. The nurse listened
to Lucy's heart for a long time and called the doctor
over. The doctor listened and nodded to the nurse.
The nurse took the baby and started walking out of
the room as the doctor walked over to Amanda.

"Your baby's heart is not beating correctly. We
are going to do some quick tests to see what is
happening."

"I need to go with my baby!" Amanda cried. The doctor held her hand and told her they would need to finish taking care of her and then they would take her to the baby.

"Most likely, the hole in her heart is taking its time to close, but we want to be careful."

Amanda's mother consoled her the best she could while Amanda's body finished the birth process. Then, a wheelchair was brought in, and Amanda was taken to her baby. They had just finished up the tests, and Amanda was allowed to hold her for a minute before they took her to surgery.

"The baby's heart is flowing in reverse. While I know heart surgery on a baby sound scary, this is not a rare event and it is a minor surgery. She should recover in just a few weeks, but she will need to spend time in the NICU."

Amanda gazed into Lucy's eyes and kissed her forehead before handing her back to the doctor. Amanda could see Lucy was a little blue and needed help. As soon as Lucy was out of the room, she sobbed. It was like she was losing Lucas all over again.

"Please, God, if you're there, let Lucy be all right. I can't lose her, too!" A nurse took her back to her room where the bassinet beside the bed sat empty. Her mom and dad stayed with her, but they all stayed quiet. A nurse came in to check on Amanda's vitals every hour. Amanda didn't answer when Juliana called. She couldn't talk until she knew her baby was okay. It was three hours before the doctor came back from surgery to let her know Lucy was going to be just fine. Amanda cried again, grateful tears this time.

"Can I see her?" was the first thing Amanda asked. They got the wheelchair again and took her to the NICU. Lucy was under a hard plastic shell with several monitors attached to her. She wore a little diaper and a pink hat. She had a small bandage in the middle of her chest. Based on the size of the bandage, the scar would probably be small, Amanda guessed. The card on the outside said Baby Weston. Amanda would write "Lucy" on it as soon as she found a pen.

Amanda spent three days in the hospital. The nurse showed her how to use a pump to save breastmilk for when Lucy was off the IV. The hospital gave a good pump to every mother with a child in the NICU to help them with the transition. Amanda stayed in the NICU with Lucy most of the day, only going back to her room for short naps. The nurses in the NICU were great about having family around to spend time with the babies. When she was discharged, though, she was only allowed to be there during the day. The nurses suggested leaving a photo of her parents in the incubator for Lucy to see. Amanda told her mom where to find the one from Alaska on her desk. The photo was taped up before Amanda said goodbye to Lucy. Her mom drove her home, and Amanda cried the entire way.

The first few nights at home, her mother stayed in the guest room in case Amanda needed her. Amanda got up to pump every two hours and often found herself crying through the whole thing. She would fall asleep crying after looking through the pictures on her phone of Lucy over and over again. It was a hard two weeks waiting for Lucy to be strong enough to come home. Each day when she got to the hospital, she found notes and gift cards propped up on Lucy's incubator. Word had gotten around about the baby who would never meet her father because he had died serving his country. They even found a pink camouflage baby hat for Lucy to wear.

Amanda was expecting the NICU stay to last a few more days when a nurse told her one morning upon her arrival that the doctor was considering letting Lucy go home that day after his rounds. Amanda could barely contain her excitement and found herself hugging the nurse. The nurse looked a little jolted but smiled at Amanda after she let her go.

"She must have someone strong looking after her to recover that quickly from heart surgery," the nurse said. "I got permission to take her out and give her a bath. Let's do that and then you can hold her until the doctor comes."

Amanda gave Lucy her first bath, and another nurse took a picture of it at Amanda's request. They got her all bundled up, this time in a pink camo blanket to match her hat. Lucy just snuggled up to Amanda and fell right to sleep. Amanda rocked in one of the chairs provided for NICU moms and just stared at Lucy. One tear fell down her cheek as she thought of how much Lucas would be in love with this little girl. He would not have wanted to name her Lucy, but she knew he would be happy about Amanda making sure she would always know her father's name. For a small moment, she could almost feel his presence right there with her and Lucy enjoying the peaceful moment. Amanda found herself smiling and closing her eyes to picture Lucas' face. It was just for a moment because then the doctor came in and announced Lucy would be his first patient that day – and she would be going home.

CHAPTER

TWENTY-ONE

A manda loved having Lucy home, but she was very tired all the time. School was out, so her mother came by at least twice a week to help out during the night. Lucy woke up like clockwork every two hours. At least Amanda wasn't having too much trouble with nursing the baby. The soreness was typical, but a lactation consultant helped her at Lucy's first two checkups and she had all the tools she needed to soothe her body and feed Lucy.

When Lucy was one month old, Juliana came out for a week and Amanda couldn't believe how big she was for only being seven months pregnant. She said she was enjoying eating for two. She brought along some ultrasound pictures and the last one showed that she would be having a boy!

"You see, our children are destined to be together!"

"We'll have to see what they think," Amanda laughed. "Maybe arranged marriages will be in fashion in the future."

"We can hope. Brian wanted me to ask you if we could give him the middle name Luke as a way to honor Lucas."

"What? Really?"

"Yes, it was actually Brian who brought it up and thought of doing Luke. I loved it, but I told him we would have to ask you."

"Oh course, Juliana. I don't know what to say except thank you.'" Amanda heard Lucy fussing, and they both walked over from the living room to her crib in the nursery. Juliana picked her up and then took her right to the changing table.

"How can one little girl smell so bad? Ugh!"

"Here, I'll do the stinky ones. You know, I thought that I was going to escape the memory of Lucas and his death by going to Spokane and living where I didn't know anyone. Did you know my plan was to not tell anyone I was married at all?"

"I wondered why you didn't want to go back home, but you hadn't told me that part."

"Now, I can't believe I wanted to do that. I now want Lucas to be a part of our daily conversation and life so Lucy can know all about him. It's completely different than what I was planning, but my heart feels more at peace with this than I think it ever would have pretending my husband didn't die."

"None of this can be easy, and I know everyone has to make their own path when they grieve. I'm kind of glad you have Lucy, though, and that you came back to a world where Lucas lives on. He loved you so much."

Both women were teary eyed as Amanda sat down to feed Lucy.

"Thank you. It's nice to hear that. I miss hearing him say it."

Amanda kept both of Lucas' parents informed about Lucy in an email every few days. Her own parents had been the ones to call them and update them when Lucy was born and in the hospital. They had promised to spread the word to the rest of the family. She sent them pictures and answered their questions about how she was growing and what she was doing. They had both sent gifts, but she was most surprised by the box of photo albums Lucas' mom had sent along with a note saying it was more important for Lucy to see her dad than for her to have the albums sitting on a shelf. One day soon, though, she'd come visit and they could scan the photos and create a duplicate album for her to take back to Florida. Amanda spent several days with the albums just spread on the dining room table flipping through the pages and seeing the boy of the man she loved. No, loves. She had pulled out the photos they had kept on the mantel and their Alaska photo book and put them on display in the living room. It would look and feel as if Lucas was in this home, even if he never got to come home. Even if seeing him still made her eyes tear up most of the time.

After Juliana left, Amanda told her mom she didn't need to come at night anymore. Lucy was starting to sleep for four to five hours, and Amanda felt like she was fully coming back to life again. Her mom came by one afternoon a week to give her a break and help with the baby and clean. A few times, she was able to run out for an errand or two by herself. Aunt Vicky came by on a different afternoon once a week, too, to do the same thing.

Amanda was very thankful that both of them were so willing to help, but they both told her it was the least they could do to help her and Lucy. They didn't say it out loud, but they all knew it was hard for Amanda to be a full-time single parent.

"Every mom needs sanity breaks," Aunt Vicky said. "People helped me, now I'm helping you. You'll help others someday."

Capt. Thomas came by with his wife once a week on Wednesday afternoons now that Amanda told him she and the baby were settled. He had made sure to call once a week like Capt. Stegner, even when Lucy was in the NICU. They always brought over a casserole. They had brought Lucy some outfits and a soft, fuzzy blanket that had a C-17 embroidered on it. They both went with her when she had to get the paperwork filled out and submitted to add Lucy as one of Lucas' dependents for the military. They gave her a list of ways their benefits would change now that there were two survivors and not just one. She put the list by her laptop and made sure to check everything over when she paid bills twice a month.

At one of their visits, Capt. Thomas asked if could bring another widow next time to talk to her about the Gold Star group they had in the area. He explained it was a group for widows and families of the fallen. They had a bimonthly support group meeting, did some outings together, and fundraised to help other military families. Amanda agreed. The following week, Clara came along with Capt. Thomas and his wife.

After introductions and some initial chit chat, Clara told Amanda her story. Her husband, Anthony, was killed when the Humvee he was in rolled over an IED three years ago. No one survived. It was three weeks before his casket came home because there was still fighting in that area. He was nine months into a twelve-month deployment. Her son had just turned two before his father had left. They were living in Kansas, but she couldn't stand staying on base without Anthony, so she came back home to Olympia and lived with her mother for two years before finally getting her own place. She found a job at her son's school district working at the reception desk so she wouldn't have to put him in daycare.

She didn't find the Gold Star group until just last year. A teacher at her school brought the group up as an organization they could support for their Month of Thankfulness. Each November, the school picked an organization to either raise money for or find a way to support to show their thankfulness. When the teacher explained that the group was made up of families of the fallen, but that they also turned around and helped other military families, Clara knew she had to find out more. It sounded like a group she should join. The teacher was new that year and didn't know Clara's story yet, but the few who did asked her afterwards if she was involved with the group.

"Not yet," she told them. "Not yet."

Now Clara was helping them by reaching out to families who moved to the area and families who'd just lost a service member. She checked in regularly with the casualty assistance representative roster and had just found out about Amanda.

"We will have one of our meetings next Friday, and I would love for you to join us. I can even come pick you up if you'd like. There's room in my car for an extra car seat, and I'm a pro at getting them in and out of cars now."

Amanda agreed to go and thought it would be better if Clara picked her up so that she knew someone when she walked into the room. She wondered if there would be a lot of awkwardness and crying when a group of widows got together. She was pleasantly surprised that the first thing she heard when she walked into the meeting room was laughter. There were several children at a back table area. Clara mentioned that the base provided two people to help take care of the children during the meetings so the women didn't need to find childcare. It was a big conference room at the base's Family Support Center and there were about 10 round tables with tablecloths, a long table with coffee, water, tea, and snacks in the middle, and a podium up front. There was a small table at the entrance to check in. Amanda handed Lucy off to Clara while she filled out the form and put on a name tag. They handed her a blue folder with the Gold Star flag on the front. Clara had a laminated one with a clip and Susie, who was sitting behind the reception table, told her they would make her one for next time.

Clara took Amanda around the room and introduced her to other people. Some people offered their story while others just inquired about where Amanda was from, if she worked, and how the baby was doing. No one asked about her husband, and it seemed like it was an unwritten rule to not ask, but listen if someone wanted to share. Amanda was glad. She didn't think she could manage to talk about Lucas' death to six different strangers.

The meeting turned out to mostly be a social event, but Amanda really enjoyed it and knew she would be back. They got some food and drink before the meeting part started and sat down. There was a quick talk by the president of the group, Sally Lemmon, and then there were a set of worksheets at each table for the group to use as questions. Sally discussed some changes to the dental insurance coverage and information on the back-to-school supply drive the base was having for lower income families. She said Gold Star families were also being offered school supplies if they wanted or needed them. There was also a reminder about signing up for the holiday cookie drive committee, meal delivery to the Fisher House, and a training team for the Air Force marathon.

The worksheet was filled with questions about ending summer well. Amanda's table discussed the first two questions about what things they still wanted to do and what their best memory of the summer was, and then the discussion veered off into more personal questions and observations. They talked mostly about their children and how they managed to do things with being the only parent and how they would tell the teachers this year about their child's father. It got easier and harder every year, one lady said. Amanda didn't say much, but listened closely, filing away their tips for later. She did share about Lucas when they all started sharing about their husbands' deaths. They all were quiet when they realized she hadn't known she was pregnant until he was gone.

"That had to have been hard," one woman said finally. "But, also, what a gift. I love that I can still see my husband's eyes when I look at my daughter."

Several women agreed. Then the conversation turned to the Fisher House, where families of servicemen in the hospital can stay, and what meals were best to take. Amanda picked up Lucy from where she was sleeping in the car seat and looked at her closely. She was still a typical baby, but she hoped Lucy would look a little like Lucas. Maybe she would keep the blond hair and have his green eyes. She closed her eyes and hoped.

On the drive home, Clara asked if she wanted to go to the next meeting. Amanda didn't hesitate to say yes.

"Are there any membership fees?" Amanda asked.

"None, but that's why we try to do things that give back to the military families around us. The base pays for everything for our group's support. Did you get the calendar with all the upcoming events?"

"Is it in the folder I got when I registered?"

"It should be. If not, let me know. There is a weekly playgroup that meets in various houses. It's a great way to get to know some of the other younger moms better. I mean younger by having young kids."

"That sounds fun. I don't get out of the house much except to get groceries and visit my parents. Lucy and I need to start meeting people."

"I'm planning to go to the next one. I think it's Wednesday. You'll have at least one person you know, like today."

"Thank you so much," Amanda said. She started tearing up, and Clara reached over and patted her hand.

"No thanks needed. We are all here to help each other."

On the anniversary of Lucas' death, Amanda finally felt it was time to look at the last thing she had from Lucas that she hadn't been able to read through yet – the journal from his deployment. She took out all four boxes that contained his memorabilia and looked every piece over after putting Lucy to bed. There were tears, but she didn't break down like she thought she might. His flight suit still vaguely smelled like him. She looked at each patch and went through each pocket. His hat was in the bottom pocket, and there was a coin in each breast pocket – one from the squadron in Washington and a coin from the one in Charleston. His upper arm pocket had a pen and pencil tucked in the pen and pencil slots and inside the pocket was a small pocketknife and a folded picture of them from their wedding. He would put his wedding ring there when he was flying, but he had been wearing it when he was running and Amanda asked them to leave it on his finger when they buried him. She pulled out his favorite T-shirts one by one and smelled them. They had all lost his smell, but she smiled at the memories of each one. His boots were on a shelf in Lucy's room. Under the books he had taken on his deployment were the three deployment journals. She put them aside and packed everything else back up. Then, she took the journals to the couch to spend some time reading through them. She glanced up at their pictures on the mantel, where she had added the framed flag from his funeral and his official military picture. She grabbed a tissue from the box on the side table and wiped her eyes.

"I miss you, Lucas. I wish you were here to see Lucy. She might just have your blond hair and green eyes. I wish you were here to hold me and that we were planning our next adventure together," she said as she looked at his photo. She opened the first journal and felt a wave of peace wash over her. It was almost as if he had sat down beside her. The first journal was different from the rest since he was just writing to save his own memories, not to her. It was fun to read how much he wrote about her. In the second journal, she could tell he really did think about her every day. There was the entry early on where he noted having been to Turkey and there were a few stars on that page. When she had asked what they were for, he had said that was the day he knew he wanted to marry her. There was only a month's worth of entries in the last journal, and as Amanda read them for the first time, she noticed a more serious tone to his writing. He spent a few lines writing about his day, but then talked about one aspect of their future each day, too.

If I stay in the military for 20 years and we have the retirement money, I would love to try my hand at teaching and do woodwork on the side. Then we would both have the summers off and could take our kids on trips like you did with your parents and maybe sell the woodwork at a few shows around the country. What about visiting every state fair through the years?

While I know I often said I wanted us to have a boy, I often wonder what it would be like to have a daughter. I see you and your father and wonder what it would be like to have that kind of relationship. Maybe we will get really lucky and have one boy and one girl. I don't know if I could do these deployments once we have a baby. It would break my heart to miss out on so much of their lives. Can't wait to start making a family when I get home.

The Ring

I just realized today that we have never been to a sporting event together. We should go catch a local baseball game and a Panthers game this year to just experience what it's all about.

My run time is really improving here. I think I'm going to do really well at the Tough Mudder. I can't wait for you to watch the race. I know running isn't your thing, but I really appreciate you supporting me and coming to see me finish the races. Maybe I should go try out a Zumba or spin class with you one day.

There was no entry on the day he died. Amanda knew he usually wrote at the end of the day. Amanda wondered what he thought about in his last moments, but she guessed he had thought of her. She wiped her eyes and picked up the three journals to take them to her room to put them on her dresser where she could read them any time she wanted. Then, she saw something shiny on the coffee table where the journals had been sitting. She didn't move for a moment, but just stared at what looked like her wedding ring. She had thought it was lost forever. It must have landed in the box when she threw it in the closet and ended up in one of the journals, she thought. She picked it up and looked it over. It really was her wedding ring. Then she looked at her hand – did she want to put the ring back on? She walked to Lucy's room and stared at her daughter. She could feel that he was still with them, even if he wasn't here in the flesh. She took the ring and slipped it back on her ring finger on her left hand. The light from the globe lamp caught the ring, and it shone for a moment. She could see the three different rings woven together and the diamond sparkled.

"I, Amanda Lynn Schaffer, promise to spend my whole life loving you, Lucas Timothy Weston. My whole heart will be forever and completely yours as long I live. I also promise that Lucy will know about you and hear your name every day. She will know you love her."

CHAPTER

TWENTY-TWO

When Lucy turned one, Amanda went back to work teaching at the high school where she first taught, and Lucy stayed with her grandparents during the day. Her mom and dad loved taking her places and it kept them active. During the summers, they started taking road trips together and tried to stop by Colorado or Florida every other year so Lucy could see her other grandparents. They both also flew up to see her at least once a year.

Lucy got to hear stories about her father from people who worked with him. Every few months for the first years after his death, she would get a letter in the mail from someone who had worked with Lucas and wanted to share stories of him with her and her daughter. Occasionally, Capt. Thomas would bring someone along who had known Lucas, and they would record that person's visit so Lucy could listen to stories about her father when she got older. Sometimes, she would be sent photos of mementos left at Lucas' gravesite in Arlington. She treasured each of these times because it meant that Lucas was being remembered by more than just his family.

Amanda never remarried and wore her wedding ring to her grave. Amanda and Lucy visited Lucas' grave every year in the summer, and Lucy told her friends stories of her father as if she knew him – because she did.

ACKNOWLEDGEMENTS

Thank you, Bill, for supporting me in my dream of writing.

Thank you, my girls, for being my best cheerleaders.

Thank you friends and family who read what I wrote and encouraged me all through my life.

Thank you Mrs. Richardson for seeing me as a writer when I was only 10 and encouraging me.

Sarah Anne Carter is a lover of books. She is an avid reader and is a book review blogger. Writing stories since she was little, she is constantly thinking of ideas that could be used as a plot for a novel. She is a journalist by trade and has written numerous newspaper articles. She grew up as an Air Force brat and married a military man and has lived in many states and countries. Currently residing in Ohio, she spends her time enjoying her family, reading and writing. *The Ring* is Sarah Anne's first published novel.

You can reach Sarah Anne at her Web site at www.sarahannecarter.com.

Please take the time to leave a review of *The Ring* on Amazon, Goodreads or wherever you review books!

Other titles by **BLKDOG Publishing** that you
might enjoy:

Dad Jokes
By K. Lee

Poems of a Broken Soul
By Iza Tirado

Fade
By Bethan White

Sacrosanct: Poems by Prison Survivors
By various authors

Lemonade
By Tom Ashton

A House Out of Time
By John Decarteret

Hour of the Jackals
By Emil Eugensen

Soft Hunger
By Lucrezia Brambillaschi

Robin Hood: The Legacy of a Folk Hero
By Robert White

Diary of a Vigilante
By Shaun Curtis

I Am This Girl: Tales of Youth
By Samantha Benjaminn

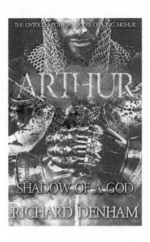

Arthur: Shadow of a God
By Richard Denham

King Arthur has fascinated the Western world for over a thousand years and yet we still know nothing more about him now than we did then. Layer upon layer of heroics and exploits has been piled upon him to the point where history, legend and myth have become hopelessly entangled.

In recent years, there has been a sort of scholarly consensus that "the once and future king" was clearly some sort of Romano-British warlord, heroically stemming the tide of wave after wave of Saxon invaders after the end of Roman rule. But surprisingly, and no matter how much we enjoy this narrative, there is actually next-to-nothing solid to support this theory except the wishful thinking of understandably bitter contemporaries. The sources and scholarship used to support the "real Arthur" are as much tentative guesswork and pushing "evidence" to the extreme to fit in with this version as anything involving magic swords, wizards and dragons. Even archaeology remains silent. Arthur is, and always has been, the square peg that refuses to fit neatly into the historians round hole.

Arthur: Shadow of a God gives a fascinating overview of Britain's lost hero and casts a light over an often-overlooked and somewhat inconvenient truth; Arthur was almost certainly not a man at all, but a god. He is linked inextricably to the world of Celtic folklore and Druidic traditions. Whereas tyrants like Nero and Caligula were men who fancied themselves gods; is it not possible that Arthur was a god we have turned into a man? Perhaps then there is a truth here. Arthur, "The King under the Mountain;" sleeping until his return will never return, after all, because he doesn't need to. Arthur the god never left in the first place and remains as popular today as he ever was. His legend echoes in stories, films and games that are every bit as imaginative and fanciful as that which the minds of talented bards such as Taliesin and Aneirin came up with when the mists of the "dark ages" still swirled over Britain – and perhaps that is a good thing after all, most at home in the imaginations of children and adults alike – being the Arthur his believers want him to be.

MORE STRANGE FACTS, UNSOLVED MYSTERIES AND TALL TALES FROM THE SECOND WORLD WAR

Weirder War Two
By Richard Denham & Michael Jecks

Did a Warner Bros. cartoon prophesize the use of the atom bomb? Did the Allies really plan to use stink bombs on the enemy? Why did the Nazis make their own version of Titanic and why were polar bear photographs appearing throughout Europe?

The Second World War was the bloodiest of all wars. Mass armies of men trudged, flew or rode from battlefields as far away as North Africa to central Europe, from India to Burma, from the Philippines to the borders of Japan. It saw the first aircraft carrier sea battle, and the indiscriminate use of terror against civilian populations in ways not seen since the Thirty Years War. Nuclear and incendiary bombs erased entire cities. V weapons brought new horror from the skies: the V1 with their hideous grumbling engines, the V2 with sudden, unexpected death. People were systematically starved: in Britain food had to be rationed because of the stranglehold of U-Boats, while in Holland the German blockage of food and fuel saw 30,000 die of starvation in the winter of 1944-45. It was a catastrophe for millions.

At a time of such enormous crisis, scientists sought ever more inventive weapons, or devices to help halt the war. Civilians were involved as never before, with women taking up new trades, proving themselves as capable as their male predecessors whether in the factories or the fields.

The stories in this book are of courage, of ingenuity, of hilarity in some cases, or of great sadness, but they are all thought-provoking – and rather weird. So whether you are interested in the last Polish cavalry charge, the Blackout Ripper, Dada, or Ghandi's attempt to stop the bloodshed, welcome to the *Weirder War Two*!

Click Bait
By Gillian Philip

A funny joke's a funny joke. Eddie Doolan doesn't think twice about adapting it to fit a tragic local news story and posting it on social media.

It's less of a joke when his drunken post goes viral. It stops being funny altogether when Eddie ends up jobless, friendless and ostracised by the whole town of Langburn. This isn't how he wanted to achieve fame.

Eddie knows he's blown his relationship with rich girl Lily Cumnock. It's Lily's possessive and controlling father Brodie who fires him from his job – and makes sure he won't find another decent one in Langburn. And Eddie doesn't even have Flo to fall back on – his old nan died some six months ago, and Eddie is still recovering from the death of the woman who raised him and who loved him unconditionally.

Under siege from the press, and facing charges not just for the joke but for a history of abusive behaviour on the internet, Eddie grows increasingly paranoid and desperate. The only people still speaking to him are Crow, a neglected kid who relies on Eddie for food and company, and Sid, the local gamekeeper's granddaughter. It's Sid who offers Eddie a refuge and an understanding ear.

But she also offers him an illegal shotgun – and as Eddie's life spirals downwards, and his efforts at redemption are thwarted at every turn, the gun starts to look like the answer to all his problems.

Father of Storms
By Dean Jones

Imagine losing everything you loved as well as the future you'd wished for so long to come true.

Seth was born with the gift to manipulate energy; unfortunately, his skills mark him as a target for one who wishes to control everything. So began a life running from those who would seek to command him, a life that spans over a thousand years waiting for the day when all will be once again as it was.

Captured in modern day London, Seth needs the help of his companions, the Mara, to show him who he is through dreams of his past, so he can save the family he has waited so long to have. A warrior bred for battle must fight once more but this time the battlefield is his mind. Can Seth win, or will he finally lose who he is and become the weapon of the man who started his nightmare all those years ago?

Father of Storms is a story told through time, a tale of love and hope where there seems to be none and above all it is a reminder that if you believe, truly believe then even from the darkest places, good things come to those who wait.

www.blkdogpublishing.com